MOONLIGHT OVER MONTANA

A SINGLE MOM CONTEMPORARY WESTERN
ROMANCE

COWBOYS OF RIVER JUNCTION
BOOK THREE

LUCINDA RACE

MC TWO PRESS

UNTITLED

Moonlight Over Montana
Cowboys of River Junction
By
Lucinda Race

Editor Purple Pen
Cover design by Jody Kaye

Manufactured in the United States of America
First Edition September 2023

Print Edition ISBN 978-1-954520-67-7
E-book ISBN 978-1-954520-66-0

QUICK NOTE: If you enjoy Moonlight Over Montana, be sure to check out my offer for a FREE novella at the end. With that, happy reading!

Jed ran his thumb and forefinger over his thick mustache then jammed his hands in his front jeans pockets. The northern bite in the air nipped his ears as he ambled toward The Lucky Bucket. A game of pool or a round of darts did wonders for working out the nagging frustration. Tonight, he needed it. He tipped up the brim of his cowboy hat and took in the expanse of Montana stars, grateful to be alive. His fingertips touched the fresh scar across his forehead, then pressed lightly against his shirt and still tender ribs. Only a few short weeks ago, he'd been close to never experiencing another night like this. The memory came back razor sharp like a gut punch that took the breath from his lungs. Polly, the head gardener at Grace Star Ranch, and he had been kidnapped at gunpoint and were at the mercy of a crazed man. Luckily, they'd survived a nightmare.

River Junction in late autumn was his favorite time of

year, especially after the harvest and before winter preparations began. These few weeks had a different rhythm as the ranch shifted from the busy summer to the long cold, and snowy months ahead.

Jed drew in a lungful of the cool night. The sharp crisp air, tinged with a bitter taste, burned the back of his throat. Smoke. He froze. Main Street was silent. Each storefront was dark. Jed walked to his left. The wind had shifted and the smell was stronger now, heavier. He jogged down the street his cell phone in his hand. Fire would spread fast here; one spark would consume the entire block. His heart pounded as the smoked thickened. A vise constricted his chest—red and yellow flames danced in the front windows of the Filler Up Diner. Maggie's place.

Hitting the emergency number, he got the address out and stashed his phone before he had even reached the front of the diner. *At this time of night, Maggie and her teenage daughter are upstairs.* He slammed his fists against the tempered glass windows, the sound muffled by the crackling fire inside. Panic coursed through his veins. He bolted down the alley boots skidding on the loose gravel. At the base of the back staircase, his toe caught the edge of a metal can nearly losing his balance he clawed the wooden rail. Looking up, his breath choked, smoke swirled around the top of the wooden stairs—the only way out.

Taking them two at a time, Jed shouted, "Maggie. Fire!" He pounded on the door as hard as he could with both fists, "Mags! Fire!"

The door opened, and Maggie stared at him dressed in sweats, her feet bare, confusion on her face, she asked "Jed, what's going on?"

"Hurry. The diner is on fire. Where's Susie?"

Her face morphed into a look of horror as the smoke drifted into the room. Her voice quivered. "She's in her room." Maggie moved down the hall and Jed grabbed her arm. "Get out. I'll get her."

She nodded and hurried back down the short hallway as Jed burst through a closed door. "Susie."

A lump of covers shifted in the middle of the twin bed and a groan reached his ear.

"Five more minutes."

He tugged on the blankets. "Come quick, there's a fire."

She threw back the covers and leaped from the bed, as color drained from her face. "Jed?"

"Come on, we have to get out of here."

He tossed a bathrobe from the bottom of the bed in her direction. "Put this on, shoes if they're close."

A look of pure panic filled her face and she froze. "I need my stuff."

He jeeked his finger to the door. "We don't have much time." The wail of sirens growing louder gave him momentary relief, right now, he had to get Susie out of this building.

Frantically, she stuffed clothes from the bed and floor into her backpack, her laptop was next and finally her phone. "The zipper's stuck!"

"Susie," the smoke thickened and he coughed. "We have to go. Now."

With a final look, she stepped into a pair of cowboy boots and he slung the backpack over his shoulder and grabbed her hand. "Stay close behind me and whatever happens don't let go."

They crept down the hall, footsteps muffled by the carpet and roar of the fire. At the open living room they froze. Maggie crouched over a duffel hand trembling stuffing it with whatever was in reach. She coughed and pulled the front of her top over her mouth and nose.

He shouted, "Maggie!" his voice raw from the haze.

She glanced over her shoulder, her eyes watering and

hesitated. Grey swirls wafted around her as he waved his arms to the back door. "Come on!"

She bolted toward them. He tipped his head skyward, and said a quick *thanks* as she raced toward them.

Jed cautiously eased open the door. *Would the stairs be on fire, cutting off our only escape?* He stepped onto the landing, testing it for strength as the flames licked the bottom steps. He put Susie in front of him. "Go fast."

"I can't." She clung to his arm as tears coursed down her cheeks. Shaking her head, she cried, "I'm scared."

"You must." He squeezed her arm and pointed down. "At the bottom, jump out as far as you can." Flames crept up the side of the building, and intense heat slapped them back.

Maggie reached out and grabbed her hand. "Susie, ready?"

Inhaling a ragged, smoke-filled breath, she choked and forced the first halting step behind her mom.

Jed was right behind them. The wooden stairs groaned and dipped under their combined weight. Ashes filtered through the air as they grappled with the bannister but they struggled to descend quickly.

They had only gone down two stairs when flames licked around the open side of the second stair. "When you get down there, you have to jump."

Neither mother nor daughter answered, but Maggie let go of Susie's hand and rushed to the next to last step and jumped out as far as she could. Once she was on her feet, she extended her hand. "You can do this, Susie."

The girl stalled as if her feet were welded to the steps from the heat. "Momma, I can't." Her tears coming faster, and Jed heard the overwhelming panic in her voice.

"Maggie, catch!" He chucked the bag and didn't wait to see if she caught it. With a grunt his slung Susie over his left shoulder, his ribs protesting under the strain. He yelled above the roar of the fire, "No matter what, don't let go of me." He raced down a few stairs and then jumped out as far as he could. He collided with the ground on his right side, taking the full brunt of the impact to protect the girl. He hit so hard it jarred his teeth and the tender bones in his body. He groaned and tried to get up, but Susie hadn't moved. *Was she hurt?*

He struggled to his knees, the girl a dead weight on his shoulder.

Maggie pulled at her, crying out her name.

Susie clung to Jed. He got to his feet and set her down while she continued to hold on to him.

"It's okay, you can let go now. You're safe." They ran clear. Distance between themselves and the burning building was critical.

A fire truck screeched to a stop and the sheriff's vehicle pulled up at the back of the diner.

Sheriff Blackstone ran over to them. He glanced toward the diner. "Is everyone okay? The ambulance is right behind me."

Maggie nodded and pulled her daughter close pressing her cheek to Susie's hair. "Scared but otherwise safe, thanks to Jed."

An arc of water fell on the flames as they continued to greedily consume the sides of the building.

Sheriff Blackstone pointed across the street. "We need to get out of the way. The fire department needs room to work."

They dashed across the street. Maggie looked back, her eyes wide and unblinking as firemen laid out water lines and kept the water pumping. The building popped and glass shattered.

Jed folded Maggie into his arms and she buried her face against his chest. "This is insane."

"Jed, can you tell me what happened?" Blackstone's gaze darted from Susie to Maggie and then finally landed on him.

"I was on my way in to The Lucky Bucket when I smelled

smoke. As soon as I knew it was the diner, I called it in and then ran to the back and alerted Maggie and Susie."

"Did you see anyone around?"

"No, the street was empty."

The sheriff nodded. "Maggie, did you close up at the normal time? Anything out of the ordinary happen tonight?"

Susie stepped into the circle of Maggie's arm and glanced at Hank. He nodded at Maggie. She said, "We had dinner in the diner just like always. You know it gets slow after seven. I had a couple of stragglers for pie, and when they left, Susie and I cleaned up and shut down before going upstairs. That must have been about seven thirty." She shook her head. "But it's hard to be exact."

"Did you see anyone loitering?" he asked.

"No, Sheriff. We went up through the inside stairs. It's a lot easier after a busy day. The fewer steps, the better." She looked at the alley. "Maybe if we had gone up the back, we would have seen something."

Blackstone didn't react and said, "I'm assuming you have a normal routine as you shut down for the night, checking the stoves and ovens?"

Jed raised a brow, uncomfortable with this line of questioning.

She said, "I've done the same process ever since I took the place over. All machines are off, doors locked, and I even check the walk-in refrigerator and freezer to make sure no one got stuck in them. Tonight was just like every other night."

Susie coughed and Maggie focused on her daughter, worry creasing her brow. "Hey, how are you feeling?"

"My chest hurts," she said as she coughed harder.

Jed pointed to the EMTs. "Let's have you get checked out."

Sheriff Blackstone said, "You too, Jed. You inhaled a lot of smoke as well."

"Will do." He guided Maggie and Susie toward the ambulance as Nina, one of the emergency medical techs, met them halfway.

"Anyone burned?"

"No," Maggie said. "Just smoke. Can you check on Susie? She's coughing a lot." She glanced at Jed. "And he kissed the ground pretty hard with Susie. Jed might need to have his shoulder looked at."

Nina took Susie's arm and guided her to the back of the ambulance and had Susie sit in the open doorway and pointed for Jed to sit on the wide bumper.

Joe, her partner, slid three small oxygen tanks in her direction. He said, "Let's get them on O2 as soon as we get their vitals, and then we can transport them to emergency."

Within minutes, Jed, Maggie, and Susie's vitals had been checked, and they wore oxygen masks.

Jed was surprised; it helped ease his breathing. But his right side ached, and his shoulder burned deep in the muscle.

At the back of the ambulance, Maggie watched the firefighters battling the blaze. Her shoulders drooped lower with each passing minute. "Our home. Where are we going to go?"

Without hesitating, Jed said, "As soon as we get cleared from the ER doc, I'll take you out to Grace Star Ranch. We've got an empty cabin you can stay in until you figure out your next steps."

Maggie glanced at him before looking back toward The Filler Up. "You can't just offer up Annie's ranch to us without asking her."

For the first time since this ordeal began, a small smile tweaked the corners of Jed's mouth. "Are you kidding? If I didn't, Annie would have me mucking stalls for the rest of my life as my only responsibility on the ranch. I'd never touch a horse again."

A flicker of life reached her eyes. "Please ask her first. I won't just show up."

"Mags, you and Annie have been friends for years; you know she'd fling open the doors for you or anyone for that matter."

"I mean it. Call and put her on speakerphone, okay?"

With the tilt of her chin, pride sparkled in her eyes and he admired her strength even more. Pulling out his phone, he dialed the house line. *Either Annie or Linc will answer and this'll be resolved in less than a minute.*

2

____

Maggie kept one arm around her precious daughter. She inwardly shuddered, what might have happened if Jed hadn't come into town. *Could we have died from smoke inhalation or worse? In a blink the diner became an inferno. Would there be anything salvageable at sunrise?*

Jed removed his oxygen mask. "That's right. I got 'em out, but the diner's still burning. I figured we could put Maggie and Susie up in bunkhouse six. It's got two bedrooms." He nodded and scuffed the ground with the toe of his boot. "Let me put her on." He pushed a button and held it horizontal. "We're on speaker."

"Maggie, it's Annie. Are you and Susie hurt badly?"

Her voice came out muffled, "Nothing serious"—she pulled her oxygen mask down—"but we'll get checked out at the emergency room. I'm not ready to leave the diner yet." She didn't need to ask if she'd have a business to come back to, the sad truth was, it wasn't looking good.

"As soon as you're done there, let Jed drive you out to the ranch and you can stay at the main house; we have plenty of room, or I'll run down to number six and make sure it's ready for you tonight. Whatever you'd like."

The last thing she wanted was to be an imposition to anyone, but one look at Susie with streaks of soot on her pale, drawn face and she didn't hesitate. "If you're sure it's not a problem, we could stay in the cabin for a couple of nights. Just until we can move back home."

"There won't be any rush, so don't worry about that. And I'll have Linc come to town. I'm sure Quinn will bring him in, and they'll get your SUV so it will be here when you need it."

Jed shook his head at her before speaking up. "It was parked too close to the building; it might not be in any shape to be driven."

She blinked away hot tears. *There was no way I'm sitting on this sidewalk blubbering for the whole town to witness. Pay attention. Annie's talking Focus.*

"Not a problem there either. We've got plenty of vehicles around for you to borrow until we know yours is safe to drive."

Nina said, "Maggie, we should get you three to the doc."

Jed shook his head. "I'll drive over. I need my truck."

She frowned. "Not the best idea, Jed—with your potential shoulder injury—but I won't argue with you as long as you let me check your vitals one more time."

Linc's voice came over the line. "Jed, don't be takin' any chances. If Nina says you need to go by ambulance, do it."

Maggie said, "Don't worry, I'll keep an eye on him."

"Good, then you come along when you can and we'll be waiting for you." Annie's voice was firm and had that "Don't question me, either" tone.

"Thanks, Annie, Linc." She swallowed the lump rising in her throat. "Susie and I appreciate your kindness."

"We'll see you in a bit. And remember, it's what friends do," Annie said. "Jed, take me off speakerphone."

"See you later," Maggie said keeping her eyes on Jed as Nina helped Susie into the back of the ambulance.

"Hold on a second, Linc." He brushed his lips over Maggie's cheek. "I'll be right behind you. And the most important thing for you to focus on is making sure you and your daughter are okay."

Joe held out his hand to help Maggie inside. Before she could turn, Jed strode down the street in the direction of The Lucky Bucket, his cowboy hat was missing. It must have gotten knocked off in all that had happened tonight. *I'll replace for him when I have a free minute.* She took one final look at her diner and home as a groan ripped through the night air. *Crash!* Flames, smoke, and debris burst out of the gaping spaces where windows had been. Her gut clenched as she shielded her eyes.

*M*aggie finished signing a stack of discharge papers while Susie waited on a vinyl-covered chair in the small waiting room. She hugged her backpack to her chest with Maggie's duffel at her feet. Their only possessions. Jed was still in an examination area. *Had he been admitted?* Maybe she could take his keys and drive out to the ranch. A few hours of shut-eye would be good for Susie before they had to face the harsh reality their entire lives were ash.

"Mags?" Jed's deep voice broke her sad train of thought. "Are you ready to leave?"

In the bright lights of the waiting room, she looked into his cool-gray eyes, crow's feet at the corners from spending years in the sun which had bronzed his chiseled face. His dark hair was cut short and a well-trimmed mustache added to his rugged good looks. For tonight, Jed Steele had been her real-life hero and she was eternally grateful to him for being in the right place at the right time.

"Maggie?" It was only when he said her name again that she realized she had been staring at him.

"Sorry, it's been a night."

"It's time to go. The truck's just outside." He slung the duffel bag over his shoulder and held out his hand to Susie, pulling her up from the chair. "Come on, kid. Let's hit the pavement."

She wrapped her arms around his midsection and sobbed, the deep gut-wrenching, heartbreaking kind, breaking Maggie's heart.

He dropped the bag to the floor and pulled her close to his chest and held out the other arm for Maggie, as if understanding they needed a minute to cry it out.

She stepped into the safety of his embrace and put her arms around Susie and Jed, and she too cried until there was nothing left but hiccups.

To his credit, he didn't rush them or try to placate them with words like everything was going to be all right. He just remained silent and held them.

Unsure how much time had passed, Maggie pulled back and in one smooth motion, he pulled a handkerchief from his back pocket and handed it to her. Susie still clung to him.

"It's clean. Dry your eyes." He ran his hand up and down Susie's back, protective like a father would be.

Maggie's gut churned just thinking of Cash Gordon, wondering what city he was in on the rodeo circuit. Not that it mattered; he had washed his hands of his daughter and her a long time ago and he was not any kind of a father to her girl.

"Sweetheart, Jed's going to take us out to the ranch. Maybe a hot shower and some rest will help."

Susie sniffed. Maggie reached out, wiping tears from her daughter's eyes cupping her red, blotchy face. "We're going to be just fine."

She nodded. "But I don't have anything to change into."

Jed gave her a small smile. "With all the clothes you jammed into your bag, I'll bet you have *something* to put on."

He was doing his best to lighten the mood, but Susie wasn't ready to go down that path, yet.

"Jed, thanks for saving us." She hugged him tight and Maggie was thankful the flood of tears didn't kick in again.

"My pleasure. Now, let's take off."

Maggie wasn't surprised to see Susie keep one arm around Jed's waist while they walked to the truck. She had been shaken to her core tonight and needed all the support she could get. Once Susie was settled in the back seat of the quad cab pickup, Jed opened the passenger door for Maggie.

He tipped her chin up with his finger so he looked into her eyes. "You're going to have a lot of help settin' things right, so don't go gettin' all tough thinking you can move mountains tomorrow. We'll need to find out what happened, why it happened, and how bad the damage is—and then I promise you, we'll get everything back the way it should be."

"Jed, you're the eternal optimist, but sometimes it's harder to set things right."

"But you're not alone and that's somethin' I don't want you to forget." He gave her a hard hug and helped her inside. In a gruff tone, he said, "Buckle up."

When he got in and the truck had rumbled to life, she asked, "Any chance we can drive past the diner?"

"Probably not. With the firehoses laid out, they're not going to let traffic through tonight. I'll bring you into town tomorrow."

"Annie said I could borrow a truck or something." Her heart constricted. *The idea of seeing the destruction in broad daylight was a lot to handle but I'd do it. I didn't have a choice.*

"Did you already forget what I said and meant? You are not the lone momma wolf with a cub in this world. You have friends. Lean on us to get you through this tough time."

Maggie didn't have to turn around to know that Susie's eyes were locked on her.

"Me and Susie have been doing this a long time together, so no worries—we'll get through this, too."

Jed clenched the steering wheel with his hands. "You've had a shock tonight and it's understandable that you're ready to dig deep and fight like you've always done, and I'm not sayin' you're not one tough lady capable of rising to meet this challenge head-on. But this time, you're not going to. And if you won't listen to me, just wait until Annie catches up with you." He chuckled a bit. "You know, you and Annie are like twins from different parents."

Maggie turned in her seat and stared at him. "I'm going to assume that is your way of giving me a compliment?"

"Absolutely. I hold Annie in very high regard." A small grin tugged at one corner of his mouth.

She buckled her belt. "Then I accept." Slumping against the seat, the last of her adrenaline evaporated. "You're right, I can see the diner tomorrow. Susie needs some rest."

"Mom, you do, too." She placed her hand on Maggie's shoulder and gave it a comforting squeeze.

Jed backed the truck out of the parking spot. "Next stop: Grace Star Ranch."

Maggie let her eyes close as Jed drove out of town. "You know, besides being strong women, me and Annie, we have something else in common."

He said, "Well, it's not pie making. Annie can't cook, much less bake."

She smiled at the truth to that statement and opened her eyes. "Annie is the first one to admit to that, but I was talking about Mr. Lucas Gasperini. Remember the guy who wanted to buy Riverbank Orchard and then Grace Star Ranch so he could turn our little slice of heaven into the mecca of dude ranch resorts?"

"I remember him." Jed's voice held a hint of reserve.

"Gasperini was at the diner today and made me quite an offer if I'd sell him the Filler Up."

He glanced her way, his gray eyes unreadable in the dash-board light. "And what did he say when you turned him down?"

"You know me so well."

He gave her a wink. "Again, remember who you're like?"

"Well, right before I showed him to the door, he said I might come to regret my decision."

3

*J*ed slowed the truck and controlled his voice so he didn't scare Maggie unnecessarily. "Did he threaten you?"

She waved a hand in the air. "Nothing like that; he said he was going to continue to make offers to the businesses around town and, either way, he was going to achieve his goals and one of those was putting me out of business."

His blood boiled in his veins. "You'll need to tell that to Sheriff Blackstone in the morning."

She glanced his way. "You don't think he would have done something like this, do you?" Her voice trembled as it grew softer. "We could have died."

He took her hand in his and applied gentle pressure. "But you and Susie are safe and we'll find out who or what is responsible for the fire. At Grace Star Ranch, you'll both be safe." Jed hoped Maggie knew he and the ranch hands would protect her and Susie if anything happened. Her hand was like ice as she clung to his. For the rest of the trip he drove in silence.

The moon glinted off the sign, Grace Star Ranch, as Jed

turned under it and drove down the gravel road. "We'll go right to the cabin and you can see Annie in the morning."

Maggie nodded. "Thanks. How close is this place to yours?"

"I'm in cabin four which is next door. Odds on one side, evens on the other. If you need anything, don't hesitate to shout and I'll give you my cell, too."

She turned to look at the passing pastureland. Despite the darkness, the vastness of the property was evident.

From the back seat, Susie said, "This was really nice of Annie and Linc, but how will I get to school?"

"We'll figure that out, but for tomorrow"—she glanced at the clock on the dashboard—"I mean today, you can hang out with me. We need to buy some clothes and heaven only knows what else."

Jed hated that her voice was filled with raw emotion. Holding back tears, anger, and disbelief were just a few that he could think she might be feeling. He drove past the main house and all the lights were on, but he didn't stop. If Maggie wanted to get to the cabin, that is what he'd do. Five minutes later, he pulled up in front of the wood structure next to his. Light shone through the slats of the blinds and the front door opened. Annie stepped onto the small porch and Linc was right behind her. Before Maggie had time to get out of the truck, Annie had opened the door and pulled her into outstretched arms, and she wiggled her fingertips in Susie's direction too.

"Group hug."

That was the last straw for Maggie as she burst into fresh tears.

Before her body crumpled and connected with the ground, Linc grabbed her and slipped his arm around her waist. He caught Jed's eye and he knew that look. Controlled anger simmered under his calm façade. Even without knowing that just today Maggie had refused to sell the diner, they both knew she was extremely protective when it came to the diner and her home. She would never have been careless. The fire had either been due to an electrical issue or something far worse.

"Maggie." Jed was opposite Linc. "Let's go inside. Annie and Susie are coming, too."

Nodding, she gave Linc a weak smile. "Sorry about the late arrival."

"Don't give it another thought. Annie tells me I'll need to get used to it once we open the resort cabins."

She took a few slow, unsteady steps before pulling herself upright, and with Jed holding her elbow, she climbed the few stairs to the porch. The door stood open, and she sucked in a breath. "Annie, this wasn't necessary." Inside there was a small fire burning in the woodstove; flowers sat on a side table, and all the lights were on, as if welcoming them.

She said, "The bedrooms are down the hall and we've got fresh sheets on the beds. The bathroom is between the bedrooms, and I added a couple of toiletries. We can get what you need tomorrow in town. I also set out some sweatpants, tee shirts, and cozy socks on the beds for you both—oh, and a fleece in case you feel chilled. When Mary heard what had happened, she put together some breakfast items and snacks and they're in the refrigerator, which is just through the arch."

"You didn't need to."

Annie crossed the room and placed a hand on her arm. "I don't need to do anything, but you're one of my oldest friends and anything I can do to help you and Susie, I'm going to do. No arguing."

Linc chuckled. "Despite the situation, just roll with all of this. Annie was the mastermind, but she used all her resources to make this happen on short notice." He pulled his wife to his side and kissed her on the temple.

"Thank you. And I promise we'll get out of your hair as soon as we're cleared to go back home."

If she noticed the shake of Jed's head, she didn't acknowledge it. For now, it was better she kept that bit of hope alive, at least until they went into town and she saw for herself there wasn't much left.

"Nonsense. You'll stay as long as you need a home." She took Linc's hand. "We're going to head up to the house, and if you want breakfast in the morning, Mary style, we'll eat around eight. But don't set an alarm to get up. You know Mary; there is always plenty of hot food any time of the day and night."

A look of confusion flashed across Maggie's face. "I thought you said we had food?"

Annie held out her hands, palm side up as if they were two sides of a scale, as she lifted one hand higher and said, "Home cooking from Mary's hot frying pan or microwaved leftovers."

Jed chuckled. "And if neither of those choices appeal to you, there is always something hearty from Quinn's kitchen."

Fresh tears welled up in her eyes and she blinked them away, but Jed could see something was eating at her. "Hey, what's the matter?" He could have kicked himself. She had just lost her business and home in a matter of hours and now the sky was beginning to lighten with the promise of a new day. And she wasn't in her diner getting ready to open to serve customers breakfast. "I'm sorry, Mags. That was insensitive." He gave her a one-armed hug. "Guys, we should take off and let these two ladies get some rest."

She flashed him a forced but grateful smile. "Thanks for understanding. And Annie? I appreciate your generous offer. Depending on how long we sleep, that will dictate if we'll be up for breakfast."

Linc said, "Fair enough and the mess hall is always open for business, and Quinn would be happy to make you anything."

Annie gave Susie a quick hug. "I'm sorry for all that's happened to you tonight."

"Thank you, Annie." She hurried down the hall and into the bedroom on the left. The door closed firmly behind her with a soft *thud*.

Jed crossed to the counter and scrawled his cell number on the notepad. "My number's here if you need anything." He gave her a brisk nod and headed for the door. Her hand shot out and touched his arm.

"Jed, I know I said thank you for coming to our aid tonight. You've done more than you had to, and I'll never forget your kindness."

He wasn't the kind of man to blush, but he could feel his neck get warm the heat crept toward his hairline. "Anyone would have helped. I was just in the right place at the right time."

She slipped her arms around his waist and held him close. The smell of smoke from the fire clung to her. With a quick peck on the cheek, she released him. "But you risked yourself to save us, and I will never forget that."

"Jed is one in a million, Maggie," Annie said. "It was fate that he was in town tonight."

He dropped his chin and cleared his throat. "I'll see you after you get some rest." He waited for Linc and Annie to walk out ahead of him and pulled the door closed.

Linc laid a hand on his shoulder and guided Jed down the front steps. They made the short walk to his porch, and Jed sank down on the top step. Suddenly, his legs felt like wet noodles. Rubbing a hand over his head, he winced.

Annie said, "What's wrong? Are you hurt?"

"I lost a good hat, and it seems I might have a burn on the top of my head."

She withdrew her phone from her back pocket and tapped on the flashlight option. "Let me take a look."

Linc stood by as if standing guard. While Annie looked at the top of his head, Linc said, "So it was bad?"

Jed nodded. "I've never seen anything like it and hope to never witness that again. I heard what sounded like the second floor crash into the first. I can't see how there will be much left come daylight." He clenched his fists. "Gasperini was poking his nose around today and Maggie turned down his offer to buy the diner. Do you think it's possible he's responsible for the fire?"

Annie gasped. "I thought he was long gone. He didn't strike me as the type to get what he wanted by any methods possible. But we obviously didn't see eye to eye on his buying the ranch."

Linc said, "And Hank and Renee Shepard didn't sell him their orchard and he kind of faded away there too."

"Do you have any plans for the cabin for the foreseeable future?" Jed asked.

She shook her head. "As far as I'm concerned, it's Maggie and Susie's home for as long as they want and need it."

He gave a short nod. "Good. With her parents in Arizona, they don't have any family around and from what I know, Susie's father is a deadbeat. I, for one, plan on helping them in any way I can."

Linc and Annie joined hands and she said, "We'll all help. But can I ask you a question?"

He tipped his head and looked up at her. "I don't need to answer that since we know even if I said no, you'd ask anyway." He didn't have the energy to give her a smile, but she knew he was quick with a one-liner.

"Good, glad we both know where we stand."

She patted his cheek much like a sister would, if he had one that he was close to. He guessed Annie was the closest he had. "What are you lookin' to find out? Something about the fire?"

"No, I'm sure the sheriff will be out in a few hours to fill us in. What I'd like to know is have you summoned the courage to tell that woman how you feel about her?"

He got up from the porch steps and climbed the last two before looking out over the ranch. This was the best view he'd ever had in his life with the barns, pastures, trees, and the mountains just beyond the river.

"No, Maggie would never be interested in me. I'm a simple guy and she's, well, Maggie." He didn't bother to disguise the reverent tone that laced his words. He gave Annie and Linc a somber look. "I'd rather keep her as my friend than lose her altogether."

Annie shook her head. "Cowboys and their dumb ideas. Not to worry, we can work on that." She gazed at Linc. "After all, this stubborn cowboy finally fessed up his true feelings."

He opened the door and paused on the threshold. "Annie, leave it alone. She's better off without me as a complication in her life." He gave a nod goodnight and went inside.

4

Maggie bolted out of bed and—for a split second—she had no idea where she was. The sun streamed through the wooden slats that covered the windows and across the cozy wool blanket that she flung aside. But the memory of her home and diner burning was something she'd never forget. Shaking her head at the ironic pun, she stepped on the cool wooden floorboards. The cabin was silent as she tiptoed out the bedroom door and into the bathroom. After she brushed her teeth, she pressed her ear to the door where Susie must still be sleeping and was grateful all was quiet. Making her way to the front room, she stopped short when she discovered her beautiful sixteen-year-old daughter curled up on the leather sofa under a plaid wool blanket. Her dirty-blond hair was draped over half of her serene face. Not at all looking like they had just lived through the worst night of their lives. But they were alive and—for the moment—warm and dry. Stuff could be replaced and the diner and their home would be rebuilt. She had insurance money and there was a future ahead of her even if it meant more hard work. The diner had finally gotten to the point it where was running smoothly after her parents had handed it over to her, and

Maggie had done her best to make her mark in the town. And her huckleberry pie was famous across this part of Montana.

She sank to the arm of a chair and inwardly groaned. There were plenty of orders for Thanksgiving she needed to bake and deliver within a fifty-mile radius. *How can I do that without a certified kitchen or a vehicle?* Real-world problems had just come home to roost.

If she was going to tackle the day head-on, she needed coffee. She padded into the kitchen, making a mental note she needed to find a notepad to make a list of things they had been able to bring with them last night, but more importantly what they'd need to get today to give them some time while she and Susie figured out their next steps.

An old-fashioned percolator sat on the counter with a can of coffee next to it. She tipped her head back and thanked whoever had made sure it was waiting for her. Measuring the grounds and water, she plugged the pot in and hoped it wouldn't take long. Next, she peered into the refrigerator. Annie had been right about one thing—they wouldn't starve. It overflowed with containers filled to the top: a bowl of fruit, milk, cream, and eggs.

As the coffee began to perk and the rich aroma filled the small kitchen area, she looked at Susie who was stirring. More than likely the smell of normalcy, of coffee, was bringing her back from her dreams.

"Mom?"

Maggie crossed the short distance between them and sat next to her on the sofa. "Morning."

Susie squinted an eye. "Why's it so bright in here?"

"No curtains on the windows. Just wooden-slat blinds."

Pulling the blankets up to her chin, she said, "Five more minutes?"

Maggie had to smile. At least something hadn't changed in the last twelve hours. "Sure. But what do you want to have for breakfast?"

"Whatever." The blanket covered her head. "Make that ten," she mumbled.

"Five." Maggie tugged on the corner of the blanket. "Breakfast first—and we need to go up to the main house. I'll need to borrow a vehicle so we can get into town and see how bad the building and my SUV were damaged."

Susie flipped the blanket off her head. "Do you think we can try and get some of our clothes? Maybe we can stop at the Suds and Fluff so we can have our own clothes to wear." She glanced at what she was wearing from Annie. "Not that I didn't appreciate Annie bringing this stuff down, but I'd rather…" Her voice trailed off and tears filled her eyes. "Mom, what are we going to do?"

She sat down and wrapped her arms around her daughter. "We'll figure it out. We always do. The Brady women are tough." Maggie felt Susie nodding and she sniffled.

A soft knock on the door caught their attention. Maggie called, "Come in."

The door eased open, and Jed hovered in the doorway. "Mind some company?"

Susie sat up and wiped her cheeks with the edge of the blanket. "Hey, Jed."

"Sure. I just started coffee if you want a cup." Maggie moved to stand and he held out his hand.

He took his well-worn cowboy hat and placed it upside down on the side table. "I'll get it."

She sank back on the cushions. *Just this once I can let someone get me coffee, couldn't I?* "Thank you."

He held up a box of cocoa mix. "Susie, any interest in a mug?"

Her face brightened for a brief moment. "Sure." It fell again.

"Hey, you don't have to have cocoa if you don't want it." Jed's voice was soft and empathetic.

"No, it's not that." She looked at him. "It's just that I shouldn't be happy about cocoa given our situation."

Maggie nodded in the direction of the kitchen hoping Jed would take the hint so that she could talk to Susie. All her attention was on her daughter even as the sound of his boots walking over the hardwood floor grew softer.

She tipped Susie's face up so she could look in her eyes. "In situations like this, we need to take pleasure in the simple joys in life. We can't change what happened last night, and if a mug of hot chocolate puts a smile on your face for even half a minute, then let's take it. I, for one, am going to savor the mug of coffee Jed is bringing to me."

At that moment, her daughter's face reminded her of the little girl who used to climb into her lap whenever she needed a momma moment. It had been a long time, but if Susie could still fit, Maggie bet that's where she'd be. But at five-eight and all legs, she definitely wasn't going to be on her mom's lap. With a sigh, Maggie tweaked her nose.

"I promise. No matter what happens today, we're going to be okay."

Jed cleared his throat and held out two mugs for them. "Mind if I join you for a cup, too?"

Maggie took the mug and inhaled deeply. She was going to take any small measure of comfort she could, too. "Help yourself."

After he handed a mug to Susie, he went back to the kitchen and returned with his mug and sat in the chair across from the sofa, tentatively sipping the hot coffee.

Once he was settled, she said, "Any chance you've heard from Sheriff Blackstone?"

"No. I expect we'll find him at the diner once we get into town." He eyed her over the rim of his oversized mug. "I was gonna drive and if there's anything you need, we can get it while we're there."

Susie said, "We're hoping to get some of our clothes and stop at the laundromat."

His brow cocked, but to his credit he didn't say what Maggie was thinking—there wasn't going to be any clothes to find.

"I'm good at carrying baskets or whatever else you might need. But either way, I'd like to help out."

She held up her coffee cup. "I accept your kind offer." Even though the last thing she wanted to do was lean on anyone, in this case it was necessary, and she wasn't looking for a handout—but rather just a little help to get back on her feet.

"What time did you want to leave?" he asked.

"After breakfast." Suddenly, she realized she was famished and there was plenty of food, thanks to Mary, in the efficiency kitchen.

"Headin' up to the main house, then?" He set his mug aside. "I happen to know there's waffle batter just waitin' for the griddle." Now his gray eyes twinkled with a hint of mischief.

Susie sat up from her spot on the sofa and said, "Waffles? Do you think there'll be bacon or sausage?"

"This is a ranch, and we're known for hearty fare at every meal. Does that mean you're interested?"

She flung back the blanket and jumped up. "I'm going to find something to wear and I'll be ready to go." She hurried down the hall and her bedroom door slammed shut.

"So much for relaxing with my coffee." Maggie got up and looked down at the clothes she had on. "I didn't grab anything before we left last night. All I took was my laptop, the money pouch, and my shoulder bag, all items I deemed essential. Oh, and my keys. Fat lot of good they're going to do me. Probably no building or car to unlock."

Jed had slowly risen to his feet. He seemed at a loss for

words. But there wasn't anything he could say that would change the facts.

"Annie mentioned there were other clothes in the closet last night, not just the sweats, and if you want a warm flannel shirt to wear, I've got plenty. They'll be long but you could fold back the cuffs and tie up the bottom like I've seen Daphne do when she's out and about."

This man, who was normally more confident, suddenly seemed shy around her. *What was that all about? The circumstances of last night, or the fact we're alone?* Now that she thought about it, this was probably the first time they had ever been truly alone, even though they'd been friends for almost ten years.

"Thank you, Jed. Let me see what Annie brought down and if I think I'm going to be cool, I'll take you up on your offer."

His crooked smile slid from one side of his face to the other and the deep crinkles around his eyes were more pronounced. She had never noticed how devastatingly handsome he was—especially with his hat off. She could see his entire face.

"Good. I'll just call up to the house and let Mary and Annie know we'll be along shortly." He placed his hat on his head, tapped the brim, and stepped onto the front porch, closing the door behind him.

Maggie stared for a moment. Did he think he needed to be outside while they got ready for breakfast? She could hear his deep voice but couldn't make out the words. Not that it mattered. Her stomach was groaning loudly, demanding food. This was the first non-holiday morning she wasn't taking care of customers at the Filler Up Diner since she had Susie. *Well, we took a couple weeks every year for vacation. This was the start to what was going to be a very hard and long day.*

The front door opened and Jed called out, "Mags, Annie

said to come up if you can't find something to wear. She and Daphne said you can raid their closets—and Susie too."

How many more times today would someone extend her a kindness that would make her want to cry? She swallowed the lump in her throat. "Five minutes and I'll be out."

"No rush."

Susie tapped on her bedroom door. "Momma, I'll be on the front porch with Jed."

She placed her hand over her heart. When was the last time her baby girl had called her *Momma* in regular conversation?

"Four minutes, Susie." She pulled open the small door on the closet and to her surprise, there were more clothes hanging than she had at home. Well, what she had before yesterday.

5

$\mathcal{J}$ed hadn't been surprised with the spread Annie and Mary had laid out at the main house for Maggie and Susie. Linc came in, as did Daphne, and it was an upbeat atmosphere while Susie dove into a heaping mound of crisp bacon, light-as-air waffles, and hot maple syrup. Jed made short work of a stack of waffles, bacon, and sausage, a couple of eggs, and home fries which should tide him over until supper. Even Maggie had polished off a plateful as well. As they lingered over coffee, conversation had inevitably turned to the fire.

Annie asked, "What's up first? The sheriff's office or the diner?"

Maggie ran her fingertip around the edge of the coffee mug. Her words came out without hesitation. "I'd like to go to the diner. See for myself how bad it is and hopefully I still have a vehicle. Then, we'll track down the sheriff and see if he knows what happened. Once I have that information, I can figure out our next steps."

"There's one thing you don't need to worry about." Annie placed her hand on Maggie's. "You have a roof over your head for as long as you need it. That cabin has been vacant for a while, and we don't need it for any ranch hands until spring."

"That's generous of you, Annie. But if we do end up staying here, no matter how long, I want to pay rent. It's only fair."

Jed could see the glint of steel-like fortitude in Maggie's eyes as he sipped his coffee and watched the two strong women basically negotiating terms for housing right in front of him. Most days he'd never bet against Annie, but Maggie Brady was no pushover. She had to be strong to be successful in her business and in raising a daughter as a single mom. He caught Linc's wink as the women eyed each other.

"Maggie, we can figure that out later. For now, let me"— she glanced at Linc and Mary—"let us give you a hand up. It's not a handout." And before Maggie could refuse, Annie continued. "I know Pops came into the diner every week and you looked out for him when I lived back east." She bobbed her head in Mary's direction. "And Pops told me how you'd always come out to the ranch and drop off a pie or cobbler when you were making deliveries."

Maggie's face softened. "I liked your grandfather; he was a good man."

"The mold he came from was shattered into a million pieces after he was born," Mary said. "And I should know; he and Annie's grandmother took me in when my husband died and after all these years, I'm still here. Generous hearts are raised on this ranch." She gave Maggie a pointed look.

She held up her hands in mock defeat. "Fine, you win. But ,hopefully, Susie and I will only be here a night or two at most. And if Mary would lend me her kitchen, why don't I make dinner tonight as a small token of thanks?"

With what this woman was going through, she still offered to cook dinner. Jed wasn't surprised. "Darlin', with all you have going on today, why don't you put that idea on simmer until you have some time."

A smile tugged at the corners of her lips. "I see what you did there with the simmer thing. You're pretty clever."

Susie said, "What time are we leaving? I was hoping I could go down to the horse barn for a while before we go."

Jed gave Susie a wide grin. "Now you're talkin' about one of my favorite subjects." He pushed back from the table. "Come on. I'll take you down and you can see Annie's pride and joy. Bowie's a beautiful palomino and she has a foal named Beau."

Before Susie had a chance to ask her mom if it was okay, Maggie said, "A quick visit. I'd like to leave in fifteen minutes."

Jed pushed in his chair and had Susie go in front of him as they headed to the back door. Over his shoulder, he said, "I'll be back to pick you up." He stuck his hat on his head as he walked outside. "I didn't realize you liked horses."

Gushing, Susie said, "Are you kidding? I love them, but living in town, it's hard to have one of my own. When I was a kid, I tried to talk Mom into putting up a shed in back of the diner, but—well, you know that's not practical."

They approached the barn and Jed slid the large door open. "No, that wouldn't have been any life for a horse." He gave a low whistle and Bowie's head popped over a stall door. "And there she is, Miss Bowie."

Gushing she said, "Wow, she's beautiful."

Jed grabbed a carrot from the bin as they drew closer to the mare.

"Can I give her the carrot?"

"Sure." He handed it to her, unsure how much time she had spent around horses.

But she held the carrot out in her flat, open palm and with the other hand stroked the golden coat of Bowie's neck and creamy white mane. "Hey, girl. You're so pretty." She looked over the stall door and said, "Where's her baby?"

"Beau's in the paddock right now, getting some fresh air. Want to see him quick before we have to get your momma?"

"Yeah." She leaned in and kissed Bowie's snout. "Bye, girl." She gave her a longing look.

"Do you ride?" Jed led the way out the back door to where they'd have easy access to the paddock and where Beau and a couple of other yearlings would be with Zak. He was the primary caretaker for them, and Jed was the lead in the breeding program Annie had started.

He stepped up on the bottom rail of the fence, and Susie mimicked his stance. He pointed to a golden foal on the opposite side of the corral. "That's Beau."

"Whoa. He does look just like his momma."

As if Beau sensed he was being watched, he tossed back his head and frolicked around the outer side of the fence, slowly making his way to where they were.

"My dad rides rodeo," Susie said. "He left when I was a baby, but Mom said he was good."

He continued to watch Beau. "I never met your dad, but riding the circuit and making a livin' at it is no place for a child."

"That's what my mom said, too. But I wonder if my dad would like me now that I'm almost grown."

Jed wasn't sure what to say, so he said the only thing that came to mind. "Any man would be proud to have you for a daughter."

"Thanks, Jed." She looked at him. "Do you think I could learn how to ride while we're staying out here? There won't be much else to do, and I'm not sure when Mom is going to let me go back to school."

"We could work something out. I'll talk to Zak Dawson. He's familiar with all the horses; I'm sure he could find a good mount for you."

She slipped an arm around his and hugged it. "Thanks, Jed. Now, if my dad ever does call, I can tell him I know how to ride, too." Her face dimmed. "Fat chance of that ever happening, though. He hasn't called in sixteen years."

The walkie-talkie clipped to his belt crackled. "Jed, it's Annie. Over."

"I'm here," he answered. "Maggie ready? Over."

"She's on the front porch. Over."

"On my way. Over."

Jed jumped down and held out his hand to Susie. But she easily jumped off the fence. Before he could walk even one step, Susie said, "Jed. I'm scared."

The tremor in her voice caused his heart to constrict. "It's okay to be nervous, but there is one thing I can promise you. And that is you and your momma don't have to go through this alone."

"Because we have you, and everyone else here at the ranch." It wasn't a question, but a statement.

"That's right." He started walking and she fell into step beside him, her long legs matching his stride with ease. "There's one thing you need to realize about Grace Star Ranch."

"What's that?" She scuffed the dirt path with the toe of her sneaker, glad she remembered to grab them in the chaos since she didn't have much else she could call her own.

"We might not all have the same last name, or share DNA that makes us family, but we are one, nonetheless. Annie and Linc are the glue that holds this eclectic group of people who have chosen to live on Grace land together as one big, boisterous family. And good or bad, kid, you and your momma are a part of that." Jed talked as if it was Annie and Linc who thought that way about the Brady women, but he wouldn't mind calling them his real family. Not that he was ever going to tell anyone, even if Annie Grace-Cooper had figured it out on her own.

"Just because of the fire?"

"No, because your mom and Annie have been good

friends for a long time and that kind of relationship is rare—sometimes better than blood."

"Like my dad."

He didn't want to touch that comment since he couldn't fathom how any man could walk away from a daughter and the woman he must have loved at one point. "Blood doesn't mean you have to love someone." And he knew better than anyone that blood could mean just the opposite.

He caught sight of Maggie sitting on the top step and his heart constricted. Despite all that she had been through in the last sixteen-plus years, she looked as fresh-faced as her daughter, and in his mind, that pretty bow mouth was sending him an invitation to be kissed.

"Jed?"

He pulled his truck keys from his pocket, trying to block out the thought of kissing Maggie.

"Jed?"

"Sorry, Susie, I was thinking about the horses." There was no way he was going to confess what he had really been thinking about.

"It's okay. Can I drive to town?"

Jed tipped back his hat and gave her a long look. "Do you have a license?"

She shook her head. "Nope, but you could teach me."

"Hey." Maggie waved her hand and yelled, "Come on, slowpokes. We need to get to town."

Giving her a side glance he said, "Maybe another time. Besides she might want to teach you."

Susie groaned and dragged her feet slowly up the walk. "She never has time; she's always working."

I understood what it's like to have an absent parent, but Maggie was a great mom and she had done a great job with Susie. Maybe she could use someone to teach her to drive, but I'll double-check with Maggie first. "I'll ask your mom, and if she says it's okay, then we'll fit some lessons in."

Her smile couldn't be any wider. "Horses and cars, a double whammy."

Jed finally understood what she was really doing. Wanting to see the horses, learning how to drive was all stalling, avoiding what was to come next. "Come on, your mom is waitin' on us."

Her gaze dropped to the gravel path. "What if it's all gone?"

"Then you'll give your mom a big hug and remind her that you both survived, unharmed." He nodded in Maggie's direction. "See that look on her face right now?"

She lifted her eyes and looked through fresh tears to where her mother was coming down the steps toward them.

"You are the most important thing in the world to her; she'd lose the diner many times over as long as you were safe."

Maggie held her arms open, and Susie ran into them. "Baby girl, why the tears?"

"I love you, Mom. And no matter what we find at the diner, we've got each other."

Jed looked away so as not to intrude on this tender moment. It was unfortunate he had never been able to say those words to his family.

"Maggie, I'll be right back with the truck." He strode down the path to his cabin and not for the first time in his life, he wished he had his *own* family with a wife and kids.

aggie's heart hammered in her chest as the miles slipped by while Jed drove her and Susie to what was left of their diner. In her heart, she knew it was gone. It would be many months before she was waiting tables and rolling pie crust for huckleberry pies in the kitchen. She reached over and grasped Jed's hand. He had been a rock ever since she opened the apartment door last night. It was the first time in her life she wished she had a partner to share a burden with, but right now he was the next best thing, and unlike Cash Gordon, he wasn't running away when faced with the tough unknown.

She wasn't about to cut Susie's father any slack. As handsome and charming as he'd been, he stuck around for getting her pregnant and then long enough for them to come home from the hospital. Three days later, he packed his duffel, loaded up his gear, and kissed her on the forehead. Without another look at his daughter, he was gone. *Why am I thinking about him today of all days.*

the pressure of Jed's fingers entwined with hers, and he asked, "You doin' okay?"

"Best as can be. Just do me one favor?"

He glanced away from the road toward her. "Name it."

The intensity at which Jed looked at her made her feel that he'd walk through hell for her.

But hadn't he done that last night? Without a doubt I can count on him. "If I start the *woe is me* nonsense, remind me I've got the most precious thing right here in this truck?"

He cocked a brow, and then it dropped.

Dang, that *had* sounded odd. She'd meant Susie, of course.

In a slow, measured drawl, he said, "You've got this. And you're right. Inside this truck, you have your daughter, yourself, and a good friend. What more does anyone need?"

He squeezed her hand, and she looked out the window before she started to cry again. The town came into view and he slowed the truck as he turned down Main Street. The Filler Up Diner was smack in the middle and suddenly Maggie's blood froze. What if the buildings on each side of hers were damaged too?

Withdrawing her hand, she buttoned up the jean jacket she had on. There was still a fire truck in front of what was left of her place and as soon as Jed parked on the curb near The Lucky Bucket and the truck was off, she pushed open the door. A plume of water streamed on the pile of rubble. Any hope of salvaging much was gone like a puff of smoke. She glanced toward each of the stores on either side and other than being covered in soot, they looked to have escaped damage.

"Mom." Susie's voice was laced with a restrained sob. "It's all gone."

Maggie pulled her into a hug close to her chest so she didn't have to face the debris. Trying to lighten the mood, not just for her daughter but for herself too, she glanced at Jed before saying, "It's okay. I wanted to redecorate anyway. You know Gram loved the old blue vinyl seat cushions."

"I love those." She pulled back, her face wet with fresh

tears. "We have to have blue cushions and the black tile floor. We'll make it just like it was, won't we?"

She placed her hands on Susie's cheeks and said, "If that's what you want, then blue, black, and white it is. We'll rebuild, only we'll add more padding to the booths. They were getting a little worn out and ready to be replaced, anyway."

Jed placed a gentle hand on her shoulder. "Heck of a way to redecorate, Mags."

She turned Susie around to face the mess and with a shrug, she said, "I'm making lemonade out of lemons; it's the best I can do right now." She gestured toward the group near the fire truck. "There's the sheriff. I want to talk to him before he leaves."

Looking both ways, she crossed the street—not that there was any through traffic as the road was one lane due to the hoses and all the vehicles around. The sharp smell of smoke filled her nose as they grew closer. It was time to face what had happened and ask how fast she could get equipment in to level it and rebuild. She sighed, *I'll have to wait for the insurance company adjuster.* It was a good thing her policy was always paid at the first of the year; there was no chance that she didn't have full coverage.

Sheriff Tye Blackstone looked their way as they approached and strode in their direction. She stopped at the edge of the sidewalk, and he joined them.

He dipped his head. "Morning, Maggie. Glad to see you and Susie are doing okay." He gave Jed the once-over. "How are you feeling?"

"No worse for wear." Jed nodded in the direction of the diner. "Tye, any news on how the fire started?"

He gave Maggie a long look before saying, "It was arson."

She placed a hand over her heart as her throat went desert dry. Dang, he didn't beat around the bush at all. "What are you talking about? Why would anyone want to burn down the diner?"

Sheriff Blackstone said, "Has anyone given you any trouble lately? A disgruntled customer, someone you've been dating?"

"First, I don't have time to date, and I'd like to think all my customers are full and happy when they leave the diner." She was proud of her cooking and service, and if anyone had ever mentioned their order wasn't up to par, she'd offer free dessert or comp their meal. Her customers always came first. That's what her parents had drilled into her from an early age—happy customers meant a happy bank account. Not that running a diner in a small western town was a get-rich-quick enterprise, but she made a decent and honest living.

He turned to her daughter next. "Susie, has anyone been harassing you?"

The girl's eyes grew wide. "No, sir."

Jed touched Maggie's arm. "Tell him what happened yesterday with Gasperini."

The sheriff's dark eyes rested on her. "What is Jed referring to?"

She stuck her hands in her jacket pockets, suddenly feeling chilled to the bone despite the sun beating down on them. "It wasn't that big of a deal. A real estate developer came into the diner; he's been in a couple of times this week. I didn't think much about it, but I knew from talking to Renee Shepard and Annie Grace that he wanted to buy both their properties. And he gave me a hefty offer for the diner. I politely declined. He left his business card and asked me to think it over and that he was staying at the River Run Inn for a couple more nights if I changed my mind."

"Was he upset when you turned down the offer?"

Maggie threw her hands up in the air, frustrated and angry at the mere thought that turning Gasperini down might have resulted in him setting her business on fire. "No, not really. He did say I'd regret my decision. He seemed keen on buying it, but why would he want to do that?" She pointed at the pile of burnt rubble. "It's not worth much like that. Besides, you haven't said why you think it's arson."

"There was evidence on what was left of the back door that it had been jimmied open. It was good you'd replaced it with a steel door. A wooden one would never have made it through the fire."

"Two points for me." She dropped her head. "I'm sorry. This is just a lot to handle right now. Was there anything else that would indicate it was deliberate?"

"An inspector will be in from Bozeman later this morning, but I have a few things for him to investigate."

Maggie didn't want to continue to dwell on arson and was grateful when Susie diverted the conversation.

"Sheriff, did any of our things survive the fire?" Susie took a step onto the sidewalk. "Mom's SUV, any of our personal items?"

He rested his hands on his belt. "The SUV is pretty badly damaged, and I don't think it's repairable. As far as other personal items, when the second floor collapsed, it just continued to feed the inferno, so I'm afraid there isn't much left."

Jed placed a comforting hand on Maggie's shoulder and Susie stood apart from them.

"Everything's gone," Maggie's words came out in a whisper and she remained quiet until the silence threatened to overwhelm her. "Why are they still putting water on it?"

"Hot spots. We don't want anything to flare up."

She understood. Now it was about protecting everything around her diner. "Can I talk to the firemen? I'd like to thank them for all they've done."

"Not right now. It's not safe for you to get that close," the sheriff said. "Maggie, I'm really sorry about this and I will do my best to make sure the person responsible is brought to justice."

"You're going to talk to Gasperini?" Jed asked.

"Yes."

The word didn't need anything more. Maggie had faith in Tye Blackstone's ability to do his job. "Thank you. For the time being, we'll be staying at Grace Star Ranch. Annie and Linc have given us one of the cabins to use as our temporary home."

He gave a brisk nod. "They're good people." Tapping the brim of his hat, he said, "Make sure to call the insurance company. As soon as the arson investigator clears the scene, you could start rebuilding."

"Thanks again, and when I'm back in business, make sure you stop in. Lunches are on me."

"That's nice of you, Maggie, but it's not necessary. I'm doing my job."

As he walked back to what seemed to be a muster point near the debris pile that had been their life, she said to Susie, "We'd better get some shopping done. We're both going to need clothes, food at the cabin, and heaven knows what else."

Jed fell into step next to them. "Do you want to drive into Bozeman or shop here?"

"I'm not going to completely hijack your day. We can find what we need for now in town, but maybe you could drive me to Bozeman to get a new vehicle later this week. I can't be without transportation indefinitely."

"Annie would be happy to lend you something in the short term so you can get Susie to school."

Maggie's steps slowed as they approached Clair's Closet. "I know, but I won't take advantage of her generosity. You know what they say about houseguests and fish?"

He smiled at her. "Quoting Ben Franklin this morning." He leaned in and smelled her hair. "You don't have to worry about stinking up the ranch, and for the record, Annie does what she wants."

"I just want to feel normal, that's all. Can you try and understand?" Once again, the tears threatened to leak out and it ticked her off. She was always in control of her emotions and took care of everyone. It was hard to be on the receiving end of kindness.

Jed held open the door, and Susie disappeared inside. "Mags, give it some time to discover your new normal. You've had a couple of big shocks—first, the actual fire and now learning it was most likely arson. I'm glad you're going to be at the ranch since whoever did this is still out there, and I'd like to make sure you and Susie are safe."

She wrapped her arms around his waist and hugged him. "You know you've made all of this bearable." His arms tightened around her as he held her close. *Dang, this felt good.*

7

*L*ater that morning, Jed carried more shopping bags and set them in the back of the truck. It all started at Clair's Closet when Clair refused to accept payment for the clothes Maggie and Susie picked out. It had been the same story at the drugstore and even at the Trading Post, which had just about everything under the sun that a person could want, and where Susie insisted she get a pair of jeans and boots for her riding lessons. He wasn't about to admit to the ladies that he bought all his jeans and shirts there; he couldn't beat the price and the clothes Jeremy Morgan carried were durable, made for a working man or woman.

Once they got back to the truck, Maggie looked shell-shocked. "Can you believe what happened today? Not one single person would take money from me. How am I ever going to repay their kindness?"

Jed turned in the driver's seat. "You're kidding, right? Your entire life you've donated to church suppers, fundraisers, given away free meals, and heaven only knows what else. This is the town's way of giving back to you. Maggie, people in River Junction love you and if the shoe were on the other foot and it was someone else who'd lost their business, you'd be in your kitchen right now cooking up trays of food to feed the firemen and anyone else who was hungry."

Didn't this woman know how special she was? A few shirts and pants were nothing compared to all she had done over the years, her parents included.

"I don't want people to think we're a charity case."

He shook his head. "Is that how you've viewed it the times you've helped others?"

She snapped her head in his direction and fire lit her eyes. "You're kidding, right? I help because I want to." The words faded away. "Oh."

Susie had been sitting quietly in the back seat before she spoke up, "Hey, it might not be the time to bring this up, but what if, once the diner is open again, we throw a big party and invite everyone in town? A grand reopening—and it will be like repaying everyone."

Maggie shook her head and sighed. "A party won't even scratch the surface."

Frustrated, Jed exhaled. "Mags, before you know it, you'll be back doing what you've always done and that will be all anyone in this town wants for you."

She huffed out a breath. "Can we go back to the ranch now? I need to make some phone calls. The first one being to my parents."

Susie leaned over the seat and planted a kiss on her mom's cheek. "Lead with the line, *we're okay.*"

Maggie smiled. "Thanks for the tip. When did you get so smart?"

A grin spread across her face. "I've spent years watching you."

Jed turned the key and the truck rumbled to life. "Next stop, cabin six."

. . .

*A*fter dropping off Maggie and Susie at their cabin, Jed parked his truck in front of the horse barn. He slid open the door and strode inside, his eyes adjusting to the interior from the bright sun. "Zak?"

A muffled response from the office reached him. He stopped to check on Bowie and noticed Beau was with her. "Hey, hotshot. Did you have fun showing off for Susie this morning?" The colt trotted over to him, expecting a nose scratch, and Jed didn't disappoint. The horse stepped closer and snorted in response as if saying he was pleased with himself. With a final scratch to his neck, Jed continued on to the office. The door was standing open as he walked in and dropped to the visitor chair.

Zak leaned back. "How bad's the diner?"

His heart was heavy when he thought of the burned-out shell of a building. "They lost it all, including her SUV."

With a low whistle, Zak shook his head. "That's rough. Any idea when we can start clearing the place and rebuilding?"

He liked how Zak assumed they'd all be pitching in because it's what folks did around River Junction. "I don't know." He wasn't sure how to add the final detail so he just said, "It was arson. Until the investigation is over, we're at a standstill."

"What are you talking about? Who'd want to burn down the diner and hurt Maggie?"

Jed wasn't about to speculate about whether Gasperini was behind this—it didn't seem like he had a strong enough motive. Although he'd been thinking about it ever since Tye Blackstone informed Maggie he believed it was arson.

"It's not like Maggie has enemies. She's one of the nicest people in town and with all she does for the community? This is nuts. Maybe the sheriff is wrong."

"We'll have to wait and see for sure; but until then, we're

in a holding pattern." Jed got up. "Are you good for the rest of the day? I want to give Susie a riding lesson and maybe have her learn how to properly groom a horse. I was thinking Nahla would be perfect. The mare's gentle and is a good mount for an inexperienced rider."

"I know Polly rode Nahla when she learned, so yeah, she's a good choice. And I can handle things for the day. Tate's around too."

Jed felt better knowing Zak and Tate would be taking care of things today. Both ranch hands were excellent with the horses. "Don't forget Doc Howard is coming out today to check on a couple of the mares. Annie wants to have healthy new babies in the spring."

He stood up. "Yeah, Doc's office called and she'll be out around two. But if I need something, I'll be sure to track ya down."

Jed left the office and walked over to Maggie's cabin. Susie sat in a rocking chair on the small front porch, her head tipped back and eyes closed. At the sound of his boot hitting the wooden step, she looked at him and her face brightened.

"Hey. Mom said you went to work. What are you doing here?"

He noticed she was barefoot. "Where are your boots?"

She jabbed her thumb in the direction of the cabin door. "In my room, why?"

"If you're not busy, I thought you might want to come down to the barn and take your first lesson in riding and care of a horse."

She leaped up. "Absolutely. Let me tell Mom." Opening the door, she flashed him a grin. "Thanks. I'm bored to tears; there's not much to do out here."

"Oh, there's plenty to do all year round. It's just a matter of changing your perspective." He wondered what she did when she was in town. But that wasn't any of his concern. Her friends were in school and she was bound to be at loose ends with Maggie busy on the phone trying to plan her next steps.

"Be right back." The door closed. Jed sank to the steps to wait. With a glance at his watch he smiled. There was no telling how long she'd take getting ready, his sister took forever at Susie's age, even if they were just going to the store. The door creaked and he got up.

"Ready to go?" But it was Maggie standing in the doorway.

Her brow was crinkled, and she stuck her hands in her front pockets. "Susie just told me you're taking her for a riding lesson. Do you think that's a good idea?"

"I've got a gentle horse picked out and it will give her something positive to occupy her time while you're living at the ranch and she's not in school."

Maggie nodded. "Yeah, she's already saying how she wants us to get a place in town and it hasn't even been twenty-four hours."

"She'll adjust; give her a little time. You've both had a rough day." He couldn't help but notice the slump in her shoulders. "Anything I can help with?"

She shook her head. "Thanks, but no. I've talked with my parents. They wanted to come back, but I told them to stay in Arizona. There isn't anything they can do at the moment."

"Did you tell them what the sheriff said?"

"How do I say that arson is suspected and it might be because I turned down an offer to sell the place? That would not only scare them half to death, but we don't know yet if it's true."

His gut tightened every time he thought about racing down the alley. As he had replayed last night over and over again, he kept thinking about what he had tripped on in the alley. The metal made a thunk now that he thought about it. Maggie would never have left trash strewn about. Which made that can a possible clue. After Susie's lesson, he'd call Tye and mention it. Better to be safe than sorry.

She pointed at him. "I know that look. The way your eyes get narrow when you've got something bugging you. Does it have to do with the fire?"

She knows my expressions? He forced his face to relax and tipped his hat back. "I was thinking about the vet coming today. We've got a couple of pregnant mares, and I am hoping all is okay." *I hate lying to her, especially when she has the weight of the world on her slight shoulders. No point in guessing about anything in the alley until I know for sure what's a fact.*

She gave him a side-eye glance. "Are you sure?"

"When I have any facts, I'll share them." That was the truth. "Do you want to come riding with us? I know you're comfortable in the saddle." Annie had mentioned in passing a while back that Maggie used to spend quite a bit of time at Grace Star riding when they were in school together.

"I haven't been on a horse since before I got pregnant with Susie." A frown crossed her face.

"Does that mean you want to come with us?"

"Not today, but maybe another time. I have to make some more calls, and if Susie's with you, it's one less thing I need to worry about. Anything that keeps her mind occupied on good stuff is a huge help."

"Then another time?" A lighthearted feeling washed over him. *It almost sounded like I asked Maggie on a date to go riding. Would she see it that way too?*

A slow smile slid from one side of her pretty mouth to the other. "Now, that sounds like fun." She took in the wide expanse in front of her and inhaled deeply. "I had forgotten how much I love being out here in the middle of the day. It's so beautiful." Nodding, she said, "I *will* take you up on that ride as soon as I get some free time." That smile seemed to dance in her blue eyes.

"You know I'm gonna hold you to that."

She gave him a saucy wink. "I hope you do. It's been a long time since I felt the wind whip my hair as I galloped through an open field."

He chuckled. "It's been sixteen years and you're already talking about galloping?"

"I'd expect it's like riding a bike. Once you know how, it comes back to you after a minute."

Color flushed her cheeks and he couldn't help think it was cute. Maybe she flirting with him. It had been a long time since any woman had, and the thought sparked a quiet hope. Inwardly he sighed, or was it was wishful thinking?

Before he was able to continue this playful banter, the door flung open and Susie rushed out, the soles of her new boots clicked against the porch floor as she approached.

"How do I look?" She twirled around, dressed in jeans, a sweatshirt, and with her blond hair in a single braid down her back. She reminded Jed of a picture he had seen of Maggie at that age on a table in Annie's office.

Maggie gave her a high five. "Like a cowgirl ready to ride."

Jed said, "Let's go, Suz." He gave Maggie a wink the minute Susie's back was to them. "And I'm holding you to that ride."

He jogged after Susie and he could have sworn he heard Maggie say, "See that you do, cowboy."

8

*M*aggie sat at the small wooden table, her laptop open in front of her, and her cell phone within reach. It had been a never-ending afternoon between phone calls to the insurance company, checking in with the sheriff's department, and talking to her parents. On top of that, she was racking her brain, trying to figure out whether she had ticked anyone off enough for them to want to burn down the diner with her and Susie upstairs. But she kept coming up with nothing. It had to have been an accident. Maybe it was all about robbery and whoever it was didn't know she never kept money in the register.

A chill raced down her spine. If that were the case, maybe the fire was a distraction to flush them out of the apartment and whoever it was waited in the shadows to rob her as they fled from the burning building. Shaking her head at the fanciful notion, she circled back to it being an accident. There was no way she was going to accept that anyone had tried to hurt them.

Shadows crept in from the corners of the living room. Glancing at the time, *Jed and Susie have been gone three hours* She headed to the kitchen; it was time to rustle up something for dinner. After being outside all afternoon, her daughter would demand dinner the minute she walked through the door. Some things never changed with kids.

Peering into the refrigerator, there was plenty of food, but nothing really struck her fancy—and it wasn't like she could serve up today's special. It would have been chicken pot pie with biscuits and she had planned to bake a triple layer cake with chocolate icing. That was always popular with her customers. Closing the refrigerator door, she sank to a stool at the counter. Her cell rang and she jumped up to get it. Maybe there was news.

"Hello?"

"Maggie, it's Mack."

She bobbed her head. Dang it, she never called him to see how he was doing. Mack had been her cook at the diner for a long time. .

"Mack, hey, I am so sorry. I should have called."

"Stop right there, boss lady. You had a few things on your mind today, and I didn't need to be at the top of your list, but I did want to make sure you and Susie-Q were okay. Rumor has it you were taken by ambulance to the hospital along with Jed and some people had ya at death's door with third degree burns and others said you were right as spring rain. Instead of lettin' rumors swirl, I decided to come straight to the horse's mouth."

"I'm glad you did, and I'm happy to report other than being checked out for some smoke inhalation, we're fine. Jed got to us before the fire was completely out of control." She rubbed the goosebumps that raced down her arm. It had been pretty close to being really bad, but she didn't want to worry her old friend.

"That's a relief. Any idea what started it?"

His question came out as a drawl so that indicated he'd heard rumors there, too. "An arson investigation is under way. Sheriff Blackstone says he's pretty sure it wasn't an accident." She wasn't going to give anything away until they knew something more certain. "Do you know if I've made anyone angry enough to do something like that?"

"No. I mean other than that guy who was looking to buy up the diner and the rest of River Junction. But with all the other *no*s being bandied about, I'm certain he wouldn't change his tactics and start burning businesses down now."

She propped up her boot-clad feet and nodded her head, then realizing he couldn't see her. "That's what I thought too. I've spent a good portion of my day replaying yesterday from the time we opened until I locked up for the night. I can't remember anyone lurking around, like an angry customer. I'm coming up blank."

"I've been trying to think back over the last few days, and Maggie, this just doesn't make any sense. Maybe it was electrical, like you left the coffee station on?"

She heard the hopefulness in his voice, and she got it. It would be better to know it had been a simple mistake and not something far worse. "I've walked through closing up last night, I can't tell you how many times. I've been shutting down the diner for twenty-five years and nothing like this has ever happened."

"I hear ya. So where do you go from here?"

"I'm going to rebuild. You should apply for unemployment and when I can figure out my next steps and a timeline, I'll be in touch. And Mack, if you need to find another job, I get it. Don't pass up an opportunity on account of loyalty to me. I wouldn't hold anything like that against you."

"Are you firing me?"

The hurt tone of his voice was unmistakable. "No, but you have a family, and I don't want to hold you back from taking care of them."

"You focus on getting this investigation finalized and when it's time to start rebuildin', I've got skills with power tools and I'm ready to work. The sooner we get started, the sooner we reopen."

Her throat tightened and she was at a loss for words. *Why was it that after every conversation, people offered to help?* "Mack, that means the world to me, and I know you mean every word." She blinked away grateful tears that pricked her eyes. "I'll be in touch soon."

"You take care now and don't you worry about a thing. It'll all work out; I just know it will."

"I love your optimism, and if I need a pep talk, I know who to call." She smiled into the phone as he chuckled and said goodbye.

Sitting on the stool, she decided that, instead of starting dinner, she'd go in search of Jed and Susie. *Maybe he'd even want to hang out and have supper with them.* Slipping her arms into a jack she grinned, she'd whip up a quick dinner later.

*M*aggie shivered as she crossed the driveway. The late afternoon air was much cooler than she expected. Withdrawing her phone, she tapped a note into the app. *Buy winter coats for us the next trip into town.* She stashed her phone back in her pocket. What they bought today were good layers, but winter was coming fast and it could snow anytime and she knew a person needed to be prepared for the cold. Heck, it wasn't even too early for a blizzard. She picked up the pace and jogged toward the horse barn. *The last thing I need to worry about tonight was any kind of storm.* Before she went inside the barn, she looked up. A few dark clouds were rolling across the sky. If the temperature stayed above freezing, it would be rain. She didn't need one more thing to happen today.

The heavy barn door thunked after she pulled it closed. From deep inside she heard Susie chattering. She pressed a hand over her heart; even though the words were muffled her daughter's excitement pushed a smile to her lips. She jogged down the wide center aisle as horses casually turned to look at the newcomer. An occasional snort greeted her and she grinned. Despite the awful day, being around these magnificent creatures gave her a sense of peach and her heart rate slowed.

"Now run the brush over her flank like this," Jed said.

Maggie lingered in the shadows, silent. Susie cautiously did exactly what he said and demonstrated on the other side of the horse. The horse picked up its back hoof and set it back down again, nickering softly.

"He likes this." She whispered as if speaking louder might spook him.

For a moment, Maggie regretted not letting Susie have a horse of her own, seeing how happy she was. But maybe when things settled down for them, she told herself, she'd ask Annie about keeping a horse at the ranch for Susie.

Jed caught sight of her and winked. The blood that hummed through her veins every time he did that was enough to push Maggie from her comfort zone to flirt back. But Cash had doused any romantic thoughts she might have had when he left her with a baby to raise and support on her own.

Jed cleared his throat. "Mags. Did you get all those calls made?"

She said, "Yes," as Susie twirled around and beamed.

"Mom, you are never going to believe how fantastic this afternoon was. Jed taught me how to saddle a horse. Her name is Nahla and she's so sweet. She just stood there while I got her ready, and then before I got on, I walked her around the paddock. Jed calls it making friends."

Maggie stepped up on the paddock and leaned into it so as not to fall back. "Did you get to ride too?"

She nodded so fast it was as if her head was a bobble. "I

trotted. Can you believe that? And Jed says I'm a natural. I must get that from my dad."

Jed said, "Your mom is a good rider, so I'm going to say you inherited that from her."

Silently, she thanked him for suggesting Susie's absentee father had nothing to do with her abilities. Even if it had put the spotlight on her. "I'd say there's something in the water around here, Susie, and you just come by your ability easily."

"Well, either way, I had a blast and Jed said I can ride anytime I want, but for the first few times, he wants either him or Zak around when I do, just to make sure. But I can come down and see Nahla every day and help take care of her."

He nodded. "Susie knows there's more to horses than just ridin', and if she wants to have her own horse someday, she needs to learn every aspect." He looked Maggie square in the eye. "If that's okay with you, of course."

That would take care of one concern Maggie might have. Would Susie be willing to feed and muck a stall as well as do the fun stuff like riding? "That's a fine idea."

Susie's grin filled her face and she looked between Jed and Maggie. "Thanks, and hanging out with Nahla will make being on the ranch a little more fun."

"The ranch has its own kind of magic, Susie. All you have to do is be patient enough to discover it."

She shook her head. "I like living in town and other than the horse part of a ranch—well, that's the only good part. It's too quiet out here and I'm so far away from my friends."

Maggie didn't want to go down this path again, so she said, "Who's hungry? I was thinking about whipping up omelets for supper."

Jed frowned. "Breakfast for dinner. I can do one better. Quinn is expecting you and Susie at the dining hall and we can head over there anytime you want." He chuckled, "First, I think Susie and I should clean up a bit. We smell like horses."

He tipped his head. "I promise, there's nothing like experiencing the dining hall at Grace Star Ranch. Quinn could give you a run for your money."

"Come on, Mom. It's kind of like going out to dinner which we never do."

Maggie held up her hands in surrender. "Fine. But tomorrow night I'll cook us all a real dinner and I'll invite Quinn, too. Or maybe he'd like to have a cookoff—in which case I'd better up my game."

Jed shook his head. "He'll let you eat his food, but he's not one to share his kitchen."

A worrisome thought crossed her mind. How was she going to bake all the orders she had for pies and other items for the upcoming holidays? It was a good thing she had the customers and their orders on a spreadsheet. The little stove in the cabin would hold one pie at a time, if she was lucky maybe two, but there wasn't anything she could do about it tonight. So, for now, this new worry was going to simmer on the back burner until she had the bandwidth to figure out a plan. "Come on, let's get ready for supper. I'm starving."

9

*A*s they walked slowly in the direction of their cabins, Maggie glanced up at the sky and then looked from Jed to Susie. "Looks like we might get snow soon."

Jed nodded. "The *Farmers' Almanac* is predicting a lot of snow this winter."

He didn't look her way, but she wondered if he was thinking it would be tough to rebuild in harsh conditions. Again, something she couldn't change tonight. So, for now, she'd concentrate on dinner and a good night's sleep. One look at Susie confirmed she was as tired as Maggie.

"I'm going to school tomorrow, right?" she asked.

"I need to check with Annie and see if I can take her up on the offer to borrow a vehicle. Barring that tiny obstacle, you'll be in school by seven thirty."

Jed said, "You can take my truck. I'll be working with the horses most of the day. No need to rush back to the ranch, either."

"That's very generous. Are you sure you don't need it?" Maggie was always surprised at Jed's never-ending generosity. At the diner, he would lend a hand with clearing a table when they were busy, helping a young mother wrangle her kiddos at Sunday breakfast, and even when the occasional customer was short on their check, he'd make up the difference. She stopped walking.

He stopped a few paces ahead of her. "What's wrong?" His gaze locked on to her, never wavering.

"I just thought of something. Over the last few weeks, a man has been coming around to eat at the diner. Usually when it's quiet. I've gotten the impression he was down on his luck and the first couple of times, he didn't have enough money to pay his check so I let it slide. A couple of days ago, he came back around, ordered the cowboy breakfast platter—you know the one with eggs, pancakes, three kinds of meat, and home fries. And when he said he couldn't pay for it, I offered to let him work in the kitchen a few days a week. Mack can always use a hand and I thought it was a great solution for both of us."

"I take it that didn't go over well?"

Shaking her head, she said, "No. He got mad and said I should be ashamed of myself for not being a God-fearing woman willing to help a fellow human being. Then he withdrew a small Bible from his pocket and opened it up, saying he'd pray for me to find empathy for others."

Jed's eyes narrowed. "What's the guy's name?"

"That's part of the problem. I have no idea, but tomorrow I'll stop in and tell the sheriff about what happened and describe the guy. Maybe he's done the same thing to other businesses around town and Tye can track him down."

"Mom, he wouldn't have burned down the diner just because you offered him a job in exchange for food. That's crazy."

Maggie could see the strain this conversation was putting on Susie. She didn't want to upset her anymore after having such a great afternoon with Jed, so she said, "You're right. I'm grasping for straws and the container is empty." She nodded in the direction of the dining hall. "We should hurry before Quinn runs out of food."

Jed snorted. "Not likely. He always cooks way too much, and leftovers end up in this soup he makes every Wednesday."

"What kind?" Maggie asked as they climbed the steps.

"Wednesday soup." He pulled open the door and Susie sashayed in.

"Right, the soup he makes on Wednesday."

A slow and easy grin filled his face. "Quinn calls it Wednesday soup. This way no one ever knows what to expect. What that guy can do with leftovers is amazing. You'd never know how good they can be, and he makes them taste like nothing you've ever had before."

"Huh. Guess I'd better plan on having a meal next Wednesday if we're still here."

He gave her a side-glance. "Not to be blunt, Mags, but why wouldn't you be?"

"I just…" The words faded away. He was spot-on. For the foreseeable future, they'd be living on the ranch.

*M*aggie leaned back in the wooden chair at the long table they were sitting at. Her plate was empty and there was no doubt in her mind that Quinn was a five-star chef and could easily take his pick of any fine dining establishment. *So why is he cooking on a ranch?* Susie had finished her meal and wandered over to the pool table that dominated one end and watched some of the hands play.

Jed dipped his head and whispered in her ear. "Relax, the guys got her back. You don't need to worry about the guys; they know the situation, and they'll watch out for her. She's got an entire ranch of big brothers or honorary uncles, whichever you want to call them. I can guarantee not one would ever cross a line either."

Relief softened Maggie's face, and she gave him a grateful look. "Thanks for suggesting we come here and not just for dinner." She patted her stuffed midsection. "The beef stroganoff was amazing."

He finished off the roll he'd been eating before he looked up. "Not what you were expecting?"

"No." She dropped her voice to make sure no one overheard what she was going to say next. "He's amazing. Not that the ranch hands don't deserve great food, but why is he here?"

"Quinn is a private man and doesn't invite idle conversation about the past—his or anyone's, so I wouldn't encourage you to ask." And then he gave her a long look and a smile tugged at the corners of his mouth. "If you do, make sure I'm around. I'd like to know what makes the guy tick."

"Does he have a girlfriend?"

His brow cocked. "Interested?"

She could feel her cheeks grow warm under his assessing look. "No. Curious. He's good-looking and if he wasn't a decent guy, Annie wouldn't have him working for her."

"True. And no, as far as I can tell, there's no lady vying for his attention."

She glanced in the direction of the kitchen door. Not that she was interested for herself since the only guy she'd like to ask her out never showed that kind of interest in her. "I'm going to thank him for dinner and offer to help clean up."

Jed stood and stacked hers, Susie's, and his plates. "You can offer but he won't take you up on it. He's got someone to help with cleanup, but the cooking is all him."

She marched over to the door and pushed it open and paused looking over her shoulder. With an exaggerated wink, she said, "We'll see about that."

He shook his head and stacked the dirty dishes in a bus pan. "It's your funeral."

Maggie eased the door almost closed behind her. "Quinn?"

He didn't look up as he scooped some noodles into a container. "Are you still hungry? I could fix you a plate to take back to your cabin if you'd like."

"No, thank you. We had plenty, I wanted to tell you how delicious everything was."

He gave her a guarded smile. "Thank you."

Dang, a man of very few words. Jed was right about conversation. "My daughter, Susie, and I are going to be staying here a while since, well, I'm sure you heard about the fire."

"I was real sorry to hear about it. I've eaten at the diner on several occasions and the food is great."

"I guess we're both fans of the other's skills." She looked around the immaculate kitchen and it reminded her of the Filler Up. "Since I'll be around without a lot to do, I wanted to offer my services in your kitchen."

A small frown came and went quickly. "Much appreciated but I have everything covered."

"Oh, I'm sure you do, but I'm used to working and until I can get the diner rebuilt, which will take heaven only knows how long, I'm kind of at loose ends."

"Again, I—"

Maggie held up her hand to stop him mid-sentence. "Before you reject me again, can you say you'll think about it and know if you need me, all you have to do is ask?"

He wiped his hands on the towel resting on his shoulder. Giving her a thoughtful look, he said, "Any chance you'd like to make a few pies for the hands for Saturday dinner? Nothing fancy, but I like to have a nice dessert our last meal of the week. Sundays everyone's pretty much on their own since it's my day off."

She exhaled and grinned. "I love making pies and you just tell me what I should pick up in town and I'm your baker. I can also make biscuits, cookies, breads, whatever else you need to go with dinner."

He laughed softly. "Don't go gettin' carried away. Pies will be more than enough help and something different for the hands. And don't worry about supplies. I'm well stocked and we got a few bushels of apples from River Bend Orchard."

Her mind began to whirl. "I could make a traditional pie, a Dutch apple, and I'm sure I can concoct a few more variations if that's okay with you." She wasn't about to overstep in his kitchen since he had just given her this olive branch.

"If you could make ten pies, that would give us some leftovers in case anyone wants a slice on Sunday."

"I thought the dining hall was closed?" Now she was confused about his schedule.

"The kitchen is, but there is always food for anyone who's hungry. Everyone knows which refrigerators are free game and what to stay out of."

She nodded and stuck her hands in her pockets. "Ten pies of the apple variety. You got It."

"Or anything else you can find you want to use. How about you swing by after breakfast on Saturday and I'll set up a space for you to bake."

She withdrew her right hand and extended it. "Thanks for allowing me to repay your hospitality."

"Don't thank me. It's all Annie and Linc, and I have to cook for the crew so two more mouths are no big deal."

"Except you might not have as much for Wednesday's soup?"

This time his smile reached his eyes. "So, you've heard?"

He shook her hand, and she said, "I can't wait for next Wednesday."

Maggie went back into the main dining room and Jed was still in the same spot. "How'd it go with Quinn?"

She tipped her head and said, "I'm baking pies on Saturday for everyone."

"How on earth did you manage to get invited into his kitchen, and to bake no less?"

"Honesty will get you what you want every time. Besides, I think he's just a good guy and recognizes I was desperate for something to do."

"Mind if I walk you home since you're basically on the way?" He set his cowboy hat on his head and nodded in Susie's direction as she yawned. "Someone's tired."

They crossed the room to the door and Susie headed in their direction. "She's not the only one. And how about I escort *you* home since your cabin is first?"

He looked down into her eyes, causing her heart rate to kick up, and held open the door. "This is a first. I don't think a beautiful lady has ever walked me home."

wo days later, Jed came out of his cabin and noticed the front door on what he now referred to as Maggie's was standing open. A backpack and pair of boots were on the top steps, but he didn't see Maggie or her daughter. He wanted to wander over there, but they needed time to get into a groove and didn't need him around.

Adjusting his hat and snapping his heavy coat closed, he heard his name. A smile filled his face as he turned around. "Good morning, Mags. I see Susie's getting ready for school." Maggie looked pretty this morning, with a light-blue puffer vest, which matched her eyes, a dark turtleneck, jeans that hugged her curves, new cowboy boots, and her long blond hair pulled back in a sleek ponytail. She had added a touch of makeup to her eyes and pale-pink lipstick on her lush mouth.

"How could you—" She grinned and caught sight of the bag and boots. "Telltale signs. Everything gets piled up before she comes flying out the door saying we're gonna be late."

"Keys are in the truck."

She crossed the porch so they were closer. "I wanted to ask if it's okay and you don't need your truck right away, I wanna drive into Bozeman to look for a vehicle. But if you need it, I can come back to the ranch."

He ran down the list of chores he had planned for today and other than the regular stuff that Zak could help out with, there was nothing overly pressing. "Want some company?"

Briefly, her eyes widened before returning to normal. "Don't you have plenty to do around here?"

"The guys will pitch in. This time of year, things are kind of slow and there's nothin' worse than hanging around, so people will be happy to help out. Even if it's mucking stalls."

Her face brightened. "I'd love company and I'll even buy you lunch if you can help me wrangle a great deal."

He tipped his hat up from his head and rested his boot-clad foot on the porch railing, as if striking a pose for a photo. "Oh, I can wrangle almost anything—cows, horses, or a car salesman. I'm your man."

"Well, then that's settled." She took a step back to the cabin door and yelled, "Susie, put a wiggle on it. We're gonna be late."

A muffled *Coming* reached his ears. "I'll meet you back here in two minutes. I just need to let Zak know he's in charge today."

"Better still, I'll pick you up at the barn and it'll shave off a few precious seconds." She bobbed her head toward the cabin. "That's if little miss can get a move on."

He chuckled and jogged down the steps and if he was a betting man, he'd be at the truck before Susie.

*A*fter dropping Susie at River Junction High School, Jed stopped at Coops' gas station to fill up. Maggie hopped out and inserted her credit card into the machine before he could get his wallet out. "Coffee's on me too, but do you need a snack?"

Typically, if he'd been out and about early, the diner

would have been his go-to place for a muffin, but this would have to do. "Doughnut, if there are any left."

She hadn't asked how he liked his coffee since it was something she'd been watching him fix for years. Working the gas pump, Jed looked down the road, away from where the burned-out remains of the diner sat waiting for the go-ahead to get cleanup started. *Maybe she'll hear something today.* Before he was finished, she came back, dangling a white bag looped around her finger and two cups of coffee.

"I scored the last two jelly doughnuts."

He grinned and gave her a thumbs-up. "My favorite."

"Why do you think I got them? Taking the day to hang out with me has to have its rewards, too."

What she didn't realize was that spending the day with her wasn't a hardship. She got in the passenger side, and he watched through the window as she put the bag on the console and turned back the plastic lid on their coffee cups. Then she placed a napkin on the driver's seat. He laughed to himself. She really did like things neat, even in a work truck.

Once he pulled out onto the road, he picked up the coffee. He had never been good at small talk and wasn't sure how to start the conversation that needed to carry them all the way to Bozeman.

"Thanks for offering to be my sidekick today. I hate shopping for vehicles and try to make my cars last as long as possible so I don't have to subject myself to this very often."

"When was the last time you did?" He glanced her way, noticing she now had sunglasses shielding her pretty blue eyes.

"Ten short years ago." She flashed him a smile as she handed him the powdered sugar-covered treat.

He placed the napkin she had left for him on his leg and then said, "Thanks." The first bite had sweet raspberry jelly squirting from the opposite side and landed with a sticky plop on the napkin. *What was she, a fortune teller?*

She handed him another napkin and grinned. "I hate when that happens. Don't you?"

"Yeah, a waste of good filling."

*A*s they drove down the two-lane highway, each licking off the last of the powdered sugar from their fingertips, Maggie's cell rang. She glanced at the screen and then at Jed. "It's Tye Blackstone." She pushed the connect button. "Hello, Sheriff."

Jed tightened his grip on the steering wheel and stared out the windshield, watching the mile markers slip by. He wished the call was on speakerphone as he was anxious to know what had been discovered.

"I see."

Maggie clenched and unclenched her right hand, so he was gleaning the conversation was worse than he imagined. "Okay, so where do we go from here?" She nodded and now her shoulders slumped. "All right. Jed and I are headed to Bozeman, but we'll be back this afternoon. I can swing by your office later if you'll be there."

She glanced his way and he nodded, affirming they could stop by.

"All right. I'll call when I have an ETA. Thanks for your help."

She dropped the phone into her lap and didn't speak for several minutes. He wasn't in any hurry and certainly not about to pressure her. When she was ready to fill him in, she would.

Silence hung heavy in the cab of the truck and after another five minutes passed, he glanced at her. Not surprising, tears slid down her face. He held out his hand and she clasped it, squeezing hard.

"It's confirmed. The fire wasn't an accident. The heavy metal door in the back had been jimmied open and the fryolator was the source of ignition. They also found traces of evidence there were accelerants used in the front of the diner. Most likely to draw attention and then once the grease from the deep fryer caught, it was out of control quickly, burning hot and fast." She wiped her cheeks with the back of her free hand. "Who would want to deliberately burn it down and with Susie and me upstairs? We could have died if you hadn't been in town." A shudder racked her body. "We came so close to—"

He tugged at her hand. "I was there, and you and Susie are both safe. That's all that really matters in this moment." Jed had a ton of questions about suspects, and he still wondered about whatever he had tripped over in the alley and Tye had said he'd let him know. Could that have been a contributing factor, too? He replayed the events over and still couldn't remember seeing a person lurking about. Whoever it was must have retreated to a safe distance and just watched.

"The upside, if there is one, is that Tye doesn't believe it's the work of a serial arsonist. I was targeted."

"What makes him suspect you were the target and it wasn't random?"

"He didn't say, but I bet it has something to do with that guy who's been hanging around the diner—the one I fed a couple of times. We'll know more once we stop at the sheriff's office when we get back to town." She gave him a tight smile. "I'm sorry to keep dragging you into my drama."

"Look at it this way… You've turned the heat up on my days." He cringed. That was either a come-on or a joke and in very poor taste.

Giving him a thoughtful glance, she said, "Yeah, I guess it's time to poke fun at the situation. I'm certainly not going to change it by being all maudlin."

Well, that was a relief—sort of. She thought he was jesting about the fire. *They needed to get on a safe topic before I put my boot in my mouth again.* "Did you look online to see what SUV you want to test drive?"

"I did and it looks like Johnson Ford has some good options so I'd like to start there first. If I can't make a deal happen, we'll head over to the Chevy dealer. My plan, is by the end of the day, to *hopefully* have bought a new vehicle and stop borrowing yours."

He admired her independent streak, but this was an extenuating circumstance. "Yeah, it's been a real inconvenience when I've been riding Tonks to not have my truck sitting there just waiting for me." For good measure, he gave her a slow, saucy wink.

Poking him in the bicep, she laughed. "You're such a smart aleck and I like this side of you. You don't let it out often." Her face fell.

"What are you thinking about?"

"I sell pies and other baked goods around the holidays and I'm going to have to contact everyone and tell them I can't bake this year. With any luck, they'll come back with orders next year since the diner should be up and running again."

"Before you do that, talk to Annie and Quinn. See if there is any way you could use the ranch's kitchen. It's got all the equipment you'd need, and Quinn isn't cooking twenty-four hours a day."

She gave him a sharp look. "Have you forgotten how protective Quinn is of his domain? Yes, he asked me to bake a few pies this weekend for Saturday dinner but I can't see him agreeing to let anyone cook in there unsupervised."

"You're forgetting Annie owns the kitchen and I'm sure with a few nice words from Polly, who Quinn thinks of as his sister, he'd see things differently. Don't forget, underneath all the gruff, he's got a good heart. Now, you might need to agree to add a few pies to the list so he can serve them to the ranch hands or maybe some of those famous sweet breads you bake up." He smacked his lips for good measure. "My favorite, for the record, is the pumpkin chocolate chip."

She looked out the side window and after a few long seconds, she said, "I'll think about it, but you have to do me a favor and not mention this to Annie or Quinn. If I decide to ask, I want it all to come from me. Understand, cowboy?"

He grinned as their eyes connected with a jolt. "Completely, and I do like your saucy side, too. In fact, you inspire me to come up with better one-liners."

She groaned as she laughed. "Heaven help us."

$\mathcal{M}$aggie hurried up the wide cement steps into the sheriff's office. Jed was beside her and it gave her the courage to face whatever she was about to learn. He pulled open the heavy glass and metal door for her and she stepped inside. The smell of old coffee and someone's lunch lingered in the air. She approached a desk with a man behind it; his badge read Deputy Barker. He looked up and she noticed his buzz-cut hair which reminded her of someone in the military. Since she hadn't seen him before, he must be new to the area.

"Can I help you?"

"I'm Maggie Brady and this is Jed Steele. We're here to see Sheriff Blackstone about my diner."

He nodded. "Ma'am, sorry about your business. I've heard the food was some of the best around."

"Thank you, and I'll rebuild so make sure to come by when I reopen."

He gave her a smile. "I like your attitude. I'll let the sheriff know you're here." He pointed to a couple of chairs on the opposite side of the small room. "Have a seat. It might be a couple of minutes."

They sat in two hard, straight-backed wooden chairs. Maggie leaned into Jed and whispered, "These are a good deterrent against crime. I wouldn't want to have to sit here long."

He grinned. "I agree." Nodding in the deputy's direction, he said, "He must be new around here if he's never eaten at your place."

His loyalty was commendable and she gave him a shoulder bump. "It's not a requirement to eat at the Filler Up if you live in the county."

With a chuckle, he said, "It should be."

She caught sight of the sheriff coming down the hall toward them. Standing up, she crossed the room and Jed was right behind her. This kind of support from him was something she could get used to, but she quickly reminded herself it was the circumstances and he was being a good friend.

"Thanks for coming in, Maggie. Good to see you, Jed." He gestured toward a closed door. "Let's talk in there in case someone comes in."

A shiver of fear raced down her spine. Based on the set of Tye's mouth and the monotone in his voice, this wasn't a random act of vandalism.

The sheriff held open the door and let them go in first. The room contained a table with two chairs on each side. Tye pulled one out and sat down so Maggie and Jed followed suit. Once they were seated, Maggie leaned forward, her clasped hands resting on the table top.

"Have you discovered who the man was that had been eating at the diner?"

"We have and it turns out he is homeless, but by choice not by circumstance. He's actually quite wealthy. Seems he's had a falling out with his family over money and said he was about to prove to everyone just how little a person needed, and he's taken it a step further to see if the kindness of strangers would pan out. It seems it's more of a social experiment than anything."

The air escaped Maggie's lungs with a slow hiss. "Now that's ironic. I help a rich man eat and my reward was my diner burns down?" She shook her head.

"After following up on the man's whereabouts, he was fifty miles away and had checked into a motel."

"So much for living a simple life," Jed said as he placed his hand over hers. "Where do we go from here?"

It didn't escape Maggie's notice that he said we, not she. Lifting her eyes, she looked at Tye. "Sheriff? If this man—"

"His name is Montgomery Johnson."

"If Mr. Johnson wasn't responsible, then who was?" Her words seem to hang in the air as she waited for an answer.

"Maggie, I don't know yet. But on a positive note, you can bring a crew in to remove the debris and prepare to rebuild once your insurance money comes through."

Her shoulders slumped. The good news faded the minute she remembered this morning's email from the insurance company—may not cover the full cost to rebuild. Bank. Loans. The words were sawdust in her mouth but she'd do whatever was necessary to save her diner.

"Thank you." Maggie stood and the chair slid back across the linoleum floor. "I've got some calls to make and if you're sure I can get rid of the rubble, that is good news."

Jed stood up. "Just one question. That can I tripped over, was it used to help the fire spread?"

"What are you talking about?"

"I didn't want to say anything until Tye had determined it was arson, but when I ran down the alley, I tripped over a can. I told him about it, and I didn't want to add more stress to you. So, I didn't mention it."

Maggie looked at the serious expression on the sheriff's face. "By the look you're wearing, I'm guessing that's a yes."

"There's a strong possibility that it was used to help the

fire spread to the front of the diner. We know the fryolator was the main accelerant, but there was more to it than just grease."

Jed put his arm around her shoulders and gave her a comforting one-armed hug.

"I appreciate your honesty." Looking at Jed, she said, "Care to drive me home so I can make those calls?"

He stepped back so that she could walk ahead of him, and he pushed open the door as she put her hand out to give it a shove. Tye followed them into the lobby.

"Maggie, don't worry. We'll find the person responsible and prosecute them."

"I appreciate your conviction, but it doesn't sound like you have a lot to go on." Wrapping her arms around her waist, she willed her body to stop shivering.

Jed took his jacket off and slung it over her shoulders. She pulled it close around her body and smiled her thanks to him.

"I'll be in touch, Maggie, and if you or Jed think of anything at all, please call me."

She nodded. "Thank you for all you're doing."

"It's all part of the job." For a tall and imposing man, his voice could be surprisingly quiet.

Deputy Barker caught her eye and gave her a small nod, his face somber. "Take care, Maggie."

"Thank you." She promised herself not only did she need to call around and find a contractor to clean up her diner, but she had to talk to Annie about using Quinn's kitchen. It was as close to ideal as she was going to get. If only he'd agree... and the last thing she wanted was for Annie to demand he give her access to his domain.

Maggie and Jed crossed the small blacktop lot. He asked, "Ready to get back to the ranch, or do you need to stop anywhere before we leave town?"

Her steps slowed. She wanted to be angry with him, but

she couldn't summon the strength. "Is there anything else you've held back from me?"

He shook his head. "I swear, I've told you all I know."

She needed to trust her gut. "Do me a favor. Don't ever withhold information from me that I have a right to know. It's about respect."

He reached out to touch her but dropped his hand. "I promise. You know everything."

She wasn't going to harp on what had happened. He had done what he thought was right. Waiting half a moment, she said, "I don't have any other stops. All I need is my computer and my phone to get things going."

"About that." Jed opened the passenger door for her. "You should walk down to the new cabins. Jessie's running the project, and I'll bet he could help you find someone reliable to clear away the debris, and Annie hired Tasha Melnick to design everything. Maybe she could help recreate the diner so it retains all the ambiance of the original but toss in a few upgrades for the next fifty years."

She hopped up into the passenger seat and leaned over to give him a peck on the cheek. "Both are great suggestions and I'll talk to Jessie and Tasha." Color flushed his cheeks, and Maggie thought it was sweet that a tiny kiss would cause that reaction. It was too bad he didn't have a girlfriend; Jed deserved to have a special woman in his life—and she'd be darn lucky, too.

*L*ater that afternoon, Maggie was walking up from the new cabins. Jed was right. Not only did Jessie know who could do the cleanup, but while she was with him, he called his contact and they'd start on Monday. A relieved breath escaped her lungs; faster than she dared to hope. Her to-do list formed in her brain. Talk with Annie about kitchen privileges, get Tasha's phone number. If she hired the architect, she'd have a better chance of controlling construction costs.

She climbed the front steps to the main house and tapped her knuckles on the door. A minute or so later, it swung open and a tiny gray-haired woman with deep laugh lines around her eyes greeted her with a warm hug.

"Maggie. It's so good to see you. Are you hungry? I just finished making a batch of molasses cookies—and the coffee's fresh, too."

Mary was everyone's idea of the perfect mom or grand-mother, quick with a hug, encouraging word, and a hot beverage. "Thanks, Mary, I'm fine. I was hoping to chat with Annie if she's in."

"Of course. She's in her office. But I'm sure she's ready for a break, too." She gave Maggie a slow wink. "And she's always up for a freshly baked cookie." Mary ushered her inside and closed the door. "There's quite a chill in the air this afternoon. How's Susie settling in on the ranch?"

Maggie followed the older woman to the heart of the home, the spacious kitchen. "She's okay. Missing our place, of course." She didn't want to tell Mary that Susie had become more argumentative, likely the stress of the situation and it wasn't like her daughter to be cranky.

"That's understandable." She nodded in the direction of the fieldstone fireplace that dominated the far wall. "Linc started a fire for me. These old bones are not as tolerant of the cold as they once were."

"Winter's coming quick." The warm smell of ginger, molasses, and rich coffee filled the air with a tinge of woodsmoke.

"Settle yourself at the table and I'll let Annie know you're here."

Maggie went to stand in front of the fireplace with her hands outstretched, soaking up the warmth. This was a nice respite after the day she'd had.

A few minutes later, Annie rushed into the kitchen with a smile on her face as wide as the Colorado River. "Mags, just in time for coffee."

She spread her hands wide. "Timing is everything."

Mary placed a plate of cookies in the center of the bistro table and added two mugs.

Annie asked, "You aren't going to join us?"

"Not this time. There's a mystery book waiting for me in the den." Mary filled a mug and slipped from the room.

Maggie stirred a spoonful of sugar and added cream to her mug before taking a sip, stalling for a bit of time since she wasn't sure how to approach the question of the kitchen.

"How are things going?"

"I hired a company Jessie knows to clear what's left of the diner and Jed mentioned the architect you hired to design the cabins. He thought maybe she'd be interested in helping me develop plans for the new diner even though it's on short notice and she might be too busy."

Giving her an encouraging smile, she said, "That's a wonderful idea. I'll give you her number and make sure you tell her that we're friends—and even if she can't take on your project, I'll bet she knows someone who will."

"Thanks." Maggie took another sip of her coffee.

Annie held out the cookie plate, "I know that face, you know, Mags. You've got something else on your mind."

Maggie took a cookie and broke it in half, setting both sides on a napkin. "I take orders every holiday season for pies and other baked goods to make extra cash. It's my holiday spending money."

"I know. Mary likes to buy your huckleberry and pumpkin pies." She patted her midsection. "They're the best."

Maggie smiled. "I'm glad you think so highly of my pies, but that's part of the problem. I have a lot of orders to fill and no kitchen to bake them in." It was easier to rip the bandage off, so to speak, and tell Annie what was going on instead of beating around the bush.

A slow grin spread from one side of Annie's face to the other. "No need to say another word. Once we finish our coffee, we'll pop into the dining hall, and I'm sure with some gentle persuasion, Quinn will be happy to share his space with you."

"Happy wasn't the word I thought of, but I'm going to offer a bribe of baked goods for the ranch hands."

She clapped her hands together and chuckled. "Dessert is the best way to anybody's good side."

Maggie grinned. "That's what I'm banking on."

12

*J*ed climbed the steps to his cabin, bone-weary from packing a full day's worth of chores into the afternoon. The guys had been busy keeping tabs on a mare in labor. The health of a foal was always the most important part of the job. He noticed the lights were on in cabin six, Maggie and Susie's temporary home. He wondered what they were up to tonight, but the last thing he wanted to do was become a pesky neighbor and drive a wedge into their friendship. *What would it be like to ask Maggie out on a date, maybe a trail ride or a movie and dinner? Hold hands during a moonlit stroll?* But it wasn't something he felt confident about. He kicked the ground, scuffing the toe of his boots. His dating skills were lacking especially with a woman who was amazing and could have her pick of any guy.

The door to the cabin burst open and Susie rushed down the steps, running in the direction of the construction site. He hesitated. *Should I go after her to make sure she was okay or at the very least careful around the construction? Or let Maggie handle whatever was going on?* He dropped to the bench outside his door and waited to see what might happen next.

Less than a minute later, Maggie walked onto the porch

and looked left and then right. She hadn't noticed Jed sitting in the shadows. Tugging a towel from her shoulder, she wiped her hands and stamped a foot. He'd seen that gesture before and knew her frustration was high. Not that she'd ever say a word to anyone about what was going on.

Clearing his throat, he said, "She ran toward the new cabins."

She didn't seem startled that he was there, almost as if she sensed him. "Thanks. I'm trying to decide if I go after her or wait until she cools down and comes back before I try to talk to her."

"Sorry I can't help with this one, bein' I was never a teenage girl."

A snort escaped Maggie. "Well, I've been one and live with one and this kid has a hot temper and one she doesn't get from me." She slapped the towel back on her shoulder. "Sorry for the ruckus."

He nodded, understanding that even with Susie's father having never been in the picture, some traits were inherited. "Not a problem. I just came up from the barn. We have a mare in labor."

"Is this for Annie's breeding program?"

"Yeah, Annie was down at the barn when I came up. As you can imagine, she's pretty excited."

Maggie looked in the direction Susie had fled. "Too bad someone decided to take off; she might be interested in witnessing that."

He stood up and crossed the small porch and stood next to the railing, closer to her and he could smell her light floral shampoo. "There's plenty of time before the foal will put in its appearance. Unless she is the kind of person who stays mad for hours." He pushed that question aside. *It not any of my business what happened between a mother and her daughter.*

"She burns hot and gets over it pretty fast. Give her a half hour and she'll be back." Maggie gave him a quick smile. "Interested in something to drink?"

"Come on over and let me entertain you. I'm sure there aren't many nights where you have sat down, kicked back, and relaxed."

"Between checking on the supper crowd in the diner and making sure a certain someone's homework is finished in plenty of time before bed, relaxation is just a word in the dictionary," she said. "I've got some munchies we can nibble on while we wait for Susie to find her way back."

Her grinned, "I like having you next door—especially if you're whipping up tasty treats. Would you like a beer or something softer?"

"Only if you're joining me. A beer does sound like it will hit the spot, and I can fill you in on the rest of my day if you're up for it."

He pointed to the chairs behind him. "Meet you there in two minutes."

She pulled open the door and disappeared from sight, and he did the same. Two cold beers and he'd even bring out a soda for Susie just in case she came back sooner than later.

Taking the bottles from the icebox, he had a passing thought of what life would have been like if he'd put effort into finding that special someone earlier in life. Would he have a son or daughter storming off while he and his wife waited for them to get over it? More than likely, given as a young man his temper had been legendary. Probably explained why he was approaching forty and single.

He heard the soft thud of boots on the porch, and he went back outside to discover Maggie had pulled a small table across the porch and set up a mini feast, artfully arranged bitesize pizzas, mini quiche, and a few other items he wasn't sure what they were.

"I see you've been cooking." He twisted the top off one

bottle and handed it to her after she took a seat that faced the direction her daughter had run off in.

She lifted one shoulder. "I had some time on my hands and needed something to do so I worked on a few new recipes that I might be able to sell during the holiday season if folks are having parties. Maybe someone would want to buy a tray of appetizers." She took a sip of beer. "I want you to taste all of them and let me know what you think, and honesty is critical."

He sat next to her and took a pull on his beer. Grinning, he said, "Darlin', there isn't anything that you've made that I haven't devoured with gusto. I'm sure whatever is on that tray won't be any different. But I promise to be honest."

"Good. Start with the little pizza." She withdrew a piece of paper and small pencil from the back pocket of her jeans. "I'm taking notes."

He did as she asked and popped the little pizza in his mouth. It was surprisingly spicy, but there was a hint of sweet which seemed to cool the afterburn. "This is good."

"It's my honey hot pizza." With pencil poised over paper, she said, "Rate it on a scale of one to five with five as the best and what was the thing you didn't like about it?"

"Four point seven five. Add a dash of red pepper flakes to amp the heat or at least have them on the side." He picked up a round of thinly sliced bread. "What's this?"

"Apple and cheddar crostini. I used apples from River Bend Orchard and the cheese is from Flathead."

She laughed as his eyebrow shot up, and he said, "I like that you're using Montana-based products. Support the locals and all."

"Fresh ingredients are key and small businesses supporting other small businesses is beneficial to everyone." She watched as he popped the tidbit into his mouth.

"It's good too." He picked up a small cup of what looked like berries in a tiny pie shell. "What's this?"

"I'm calling it huckleberry bacon tart. It has a couple of kinds of cheese, bacon, and huckleberries." Something in the distance drew her attention, but she continued by saying, "I've been playing around with the concept so it might not be that great."

He bit it in half and chewed slowly. There was a sweet, smoky tang that proceeded the crunch of the flaky crust. He ate the other half quickly and then one more. "Mags, this is a five plus. I hope you wrote the recipe down since this is the best of the bunch."

Her eyes widened and she smiled. "What makes this one a hit over the others?"

"I'm a sucker for berries and bacon and the cheese has a sharpness to it that offsets both. Now, remember I'm not a gourmet; I just like dang good food."

Her focus was still laser-like on the darkness beyond the porch and he guessed it was Susie.

"So that one is definitely a keeper?"

"They all are, but that is my favorite. In fact, I'll sample a couple more just to make sure."

She laughed softly but she didn't look at him. From the corner of his eye, he could see Susie emerge from the darkness. As she drew closer, he could see her face was blotchy and her eyes were red, too.

Stopping at the bottom of the porch steps, she said, "Hey."

Jed held up the soft drink. "Just in time."

Her sneakers didn't make a sound on the wooden steps as she took the can. "Thanks." Perching on the porch railing, she popped the top with a snap. "Any more snacks?"

"Plenty. I'll just go next door and refill the tray."

Maggie stood, but Susie said, "I'll go, Mom." She set the can down and picked up the tray. "Does anyone need anything else?"

"I think we're all set," Maggie said and he nodded in agreement.

When she closed the door to their cabin behind her, Jed flashed a look at Maggie, his eyebrow arched in question.

"This is her way. When she comes back, she'll apologize and we'll talk about what happened later."

He went to get up. "I'll go inside."

"No, please. Stay. Besides, after she eats something, we could go down to the barn if you still think it's a good idea."

"We can do that. But I haven't wanted to ask what happened. If you want to talk about it, I can be a good sounding board."

She glanced at the other cabin. "In a nutshell she hates the ranch and wants to go back to town. I think in some way she's blaming me for the fire."

"How can she? Arson is a crime and it's not like you set your place ablaze." He did his best to temper back his annoyance.

"It's not really about what I did or didn't do. It's a reaction to her losing everything and the reality of what might have happened has hit her hard."

He could understand that. A few more minutes and he might not have been able to get up the stairs to save them and that made his blood freeze in his veins.

Susie came back up the porch steps and held the tray out to Jed and Maggie before she set it down. "Mom, I'm sorry about before. I didn't mean what I said, and I know this isn't your fault. I just miss being at our house, with our stuff." She sniffed and pressed her fingertips to her eyes. "I want to go home."

Maggie got up and pulled her close. "And we will as soon as we rebuild—and this time, we'll design the upstairs exactly as we want. And maybe it won't be that long, but I need for you to be patient. We're in this together."

Jed shifted in his seat. If he could slip into the cabin and give them some privacy, he would, but it would be more awkward if he moved and interrupted their conversation so he stayed put.

"Now, dry your eyes and eat since Jed has something really cool to show you."

Susie gave him a weak smile. "Sorry about all this."

"Think nothing of it, but you might want to get a jacket. We're going down to the barn. There's a mare in labor and with any luck you might get to witness a new life coming into our world."

Her face brightened. "Like now?"

He laughed. "Soon, but you have time."

She turned to Maggie. "Is it okay, Mom?"

Cupping Susie's cheek, she said, "We'll go together. But Jed's right; we need jackets. I'm sure it's going to get cold."

Susie picked up a handful of appetizers and raced back to their cabin, "Mom, I'll grab your jacket."

"I guess there is a small benefit to ranch life."

Maggie nodded. "She couldn't see a foal being born if we were home. Maybe when she starts to realize all the interesting things that happen on a ranch, she'll enjoy the experience instead of fighting me every step of the way."

Jed had a feeling tonight's fight hadn't been the first and if he were a betting man, it wouldn't be the last, either.

He took the last swallow of his beer and popped another tart in his mouth. "When we come back up, I want to hear what happened with the rest of your day."

She gave him a slow assessing smile. "Let's just say I got a lot accomplished and it's all thanks to you."

13

*B*y the time they reached Jed's cabin Maggie was bone weary. But she wanted to fill him in on all that had happened today—well, really yesterday—since it was directly related to his encouragement.

Susie dropped to the top step. "Can you believe we just witnessed a filly born and she's so pretty. She almost looks gold."

"Annie is breeding palominos and they have yellow to gold coats with a white mane and tail, and their eyes are a deep brown. With our horses here, we're breeding quarter horses that are calm and good disposition unlike their Arabian cousins which can be high-strung and more spirited. But Annie is looking not just for coloring, but temperament too."

"Could a palomino be a good rodeo horse?"

"Ours could be a good choice since a quarter horse has lightning-fast reflexes and are very athletic which makes them highly competitive on the rodeo circuit."

Maggie was pleased that Jed was taking his time to explain the differences and she said, "What makes you ask about the rodeo? Thinking of running away and joining up?"

Susie laughed. "Mom, I barely know how to ride a horse, let alone be ready to barrel race or anything. I was just curious since my—" She stopped talking and got up. "I'm going to bed. Wait until I tell everyone at school what happened tonight. I'll bet none of them got to see a baby horse born."

Jed said, "Good night, Susie. Feel free to come down to the barn tomorrow when you get home from school."

"Any chance for a riding lesson?"

Maggie could hear the hopeful tone in her voice. Before she could tell her daughter Jed had a job to do, he interjected. "I'm sure we can work something out. But there might be a few barn chores involved."

"I'll do anything, even muck stalls."

He chuckled. "I'll keep that in mind."

Susie pecked Maggie's cheek and said good night before disappearing inside their cabin.

"Jed, if you're busy, don't feel you need to take time out of your day to give her a lesson."

He gestured for her to sit down, and he leaned back in the same chair he had been in earlier. "Mags, just to be clear, I don't do anything I don't want to do. And showing Susie the ropes for riding and caring for a horse might help to ease the tension between the two of you while you're living out here."

His deep, rich voice was a balm to her ragged soul. She exhaled. "It really is pretty out here this time of night."

"Technically, it's morning, very early, but it still counts."

She took several deep cleansing breaths. "To pick up on our earlier conversation, I talked to Jesse and got in touch with a crew that will clean the debris away and get us to square one, and Annie gave me Tasha Melnick's business card. I reached out to her and she's going to meet me tomorrow around nine at the diner. Even though it's still a mess over there, I want to show her some pictures and have her get a feel for the town."

"Solid plan. Now, what about the matter of you lacking a commercial kitchen?"

The light was too dim to see his face, but she'd hazard a guess his brow cocked like it usually did when he asked a question that needed more than just a quick answer.

She rubbed her hands together to warm them and stuck them into her fleece pockets. "Good news there, too. I talked with Annie and she went down with me to see Quinn. I had to promise I would bake one day a week for the ranch hands which will lighten his load in exchange for kitchen privileges."

"Sounds fair and the hands will go nuts over your pies and cakes. Quinn's a great chef and he's good at desserts, but they don't compare to yours."

"The last few days have seemed like months—but with everyone being so generous and supportive, it's made this bearable." Maggie had always known she was lucky to live in the small ranching community of River Junction and did her best to be a good neighbor, but never in a million years would she have guessed she'd be the one who needed help.

He reached over and placed a hand on her arm. "I can guarantee people helping out isn't over, either."

She blinked away the tears that she wanted to save for when she was alone in the shower.

He squeezed her arm gently. "Everyone loves you and no one wants to see you or Susie suffer any more than you already have. Losing everything in that fire? Well, I can't even begin to grasp how you must feel—and on top of it, that it was deliberate."

"That's something that scares me. What if Tye Blackstone can't find who did it and they come back for another go at my diner after it's rebuilt?"

"That won't happen for two reasons. Tye is good at his job, and this time around you'll have state-of-the-art security cameras and a fire suppression system. With the new construction, you'll have to meet the new building codes."

Her gut clenched. That sounded very expensive even if it was necessary. "How will a security system help?"

"I've seen what Annie has around here. Linc installed it after Polly and I were kidnapped, and if anything triggers a camera, they get an alert on their cell phone. It's slick and you don't have to be glued to a monitor. If you have questions about how it all works, I'm sure Annie would fill you in on the details."

"You know, I've never told you how impressed I was knowing you tried to save Polly from that crazy man. You're a good friend."

With a snort, he said, "Yeah, but did you hear? She ended up saving us both. I was hog-tied and not much help to her when we were in that cave. I was able to cut her hands free but that was it."

"You had a concussion, so cut yourself some slack. The best thing you did for her was show up. Who knows what might have happened to her if you didn't come along and slow the whole kidnapping down. He might have killed her before nightfall."

In the faint gray of the coming dawn, she watched as he rubbed a hand over his face. Weary-worn, not from the night that had just happened, but haunted by the memory of that horrible event. Anyone would have felt helpless, and Maggie could tell by the dip of his chin and slump of his shoulders he carried that burden every day. "Have you talked to Polly about what happened?"

"No."

He got very quiet and she waited. Sometimes silence with a friend helped more than anything.

"I was coming up from the barn, headed to the dining hall when I saw Polly coming down from the greenhouse and he was with her, not touching her but the expression she wore confirmed things weren't quite right. We had started to carry handguns from the mountain lion incident and when I reached for my gun, I remembered I'd taken it off when I was in the barn. I sauntered over with a big stupid grin on my face the entire time my brain was racing on what I could use as a weapon if needed. But sadly, there was nothing."

Her heart ached for him, and she understood the helplessness that must have washed over him. It probably compared to the split second it registered the diner was burning down around her.

"When I was a couple of feet away from them, Polly started yelling at me like we were in the midst of an argument. Telling me I was a jerk and if she had wanted an apology, she would have come lookin' for me. Told me to beat boots."

"Had you been arguing?"

"No. That's not her way. She talks everything out in a calm and easy manner. Even when Clint does something to annoy her, you can see them sit someplace, heads together, and before long they're smiling again. It's the best part about her. That's when I knew."

"At this point you're standing between them and the car?"

"Yup. That's when I noticed the gun was pressed into her side. He told me to get in the car and if I didn't, she'd be dead before she kissed the dirt."

Her hand flew to her mouth. She had never heard this part of the story and each sentence Jed said painted a picture of no way out.

"He gestured to the car and told me to pop the trunk and get in. I turned and that's the last thing I remember until waking up in the cave with the worst headache of my life."

She dropped to one knee in front of him and took his hands in hers. "It wasn't your fault and you need to talk to Polly. I'm sure she doesn't blame you, either."

He squeezed her hands as if hanging on for dear life. This

was the first time she'd ever seen this side of Jed, vulnerable and needing someone. "How about I make us all breakfast. You can come over and fix coffee. I'll take Susie to school, meet with Tasha, and we can catch up later."

"Thanks, but I need to get an hour of sleep and so do you. It's going to be a busy day for both of us and the last thing you need is some long-faced cowboy hanging around." He leaned forward and kissed her forehead. "I appreciate you listening and please don't tell anyone about this conversation."

"I'll let you go inside on one condition." She pulled the tall, lanky man to his feet. "Talk to Polly. I won't bring it up again, but promise me you'll think about it."

He wrapped his arms around her and drew her close to his broad chest, her five-foot-five frame fitting just perfectly there. As he held her tight, she felt all would be okay for them both.

"Come find me later. I want to hear all about the plans for the diner." He took a step back as he released her from his arms. "You're a good friend, Mags."

She looked up into his steel-gray eyes. "Takes one to know one, Jed. Sleep well."

14

"**H**ow's our new girl doing?" Linc strode down the center of the barn with a mile-wide grin.

Jed looked up from leaning against the stall, watching the filly. "She's looking good. Doc Howard will be out later to check her over, but I think she's gonna make a fine addition to the future of Grace Star Ranch. I'm surprised Annie's not with you." The wonder of new life always struck him with longing for what might have been if his life had been different. But he was content.

Linc chuckled and he leaned against the stall, looking at the filly and her mama. "She'll be down soon, but she and Daphne had a few things to go over for the dude ranch operation."

Daphne Brenner was Annie's best friend from boarding school who moved out here from Boston almost two years ago, where she had worked as a wedding planner, to run the guest portion of the ranch. With the cabins almost complete, the plan was to be open in the spring. "I heard Daphne talking with Quinn last week and it sounds like they're going to expand the kitchen staff and the guests will be able to eat in the dining hall with the ranch hands."

"Daphne and Annie think it's the best way to give the guests a full ranch life experience, but there will still be plenty of luxury. Annie added an outdoor pavilion and kitchen closer to the cabins and Quinn knows a guy who only cooks over fire so talks are open to bring him here for the summer months for dinners."

Jed gave Linc a long look. "Will the ranch hands be excluded?"

"You know how my bride feels about the men and women who work the ranch; they're family…and if we're doing a barbeque in the new area or serving a turkey dinner in the hall, everyone is welcome." Linc clapped his hand on Jed's shoulder. "What's eatin' you?"

He pushed back his cowboy hat. "Tired. Long night waitin' on that little girl."

"Are you sure it's not the woman and her daughter living next to you that's keeping you up at night? It's not a secret to anyone who's seen you two together that you care for her."

Keeping his voice even, he said, "Maggie's my friend and both she and Susie have been through a lot."

"I've heard and said that *she's a friend* line before. Look at what happened to me and Clint. Our 'friends'"—he used air quotes around friends—"are now our wives."

"There's no way I'll be getting down on one knee. I'm too old and set in my ways to ask any woman to marry me. Besides, I'd never want to live anywhere but this ranch. It's the first real home I've ever had where I'm happy and she has her life in town. It'll never work out, anyway."

Chuckling, Linc said, "Oh, Jed, you sound more like me every time you speak. And now look at me, a man happily married to the love of his life. Life doesn't get much sweeter than this."

Jed gave him a sharp look as a stab of envy pierced his heart. "I'm happy for you. She's a good person."

He waved a hand around his face. "You, too, can walk

around wearing a cocky grin on your mug if you'd cowboy up and ask the woman out on a date."

"Yeah, that's not gonna happen. She's got too much going on and Susie's not happy out here, so she might just end up renting a place in town."

"Single mom and a business owner. She *does* have a lot on her plate, but I heard you're teaching Susie to ride—so that must take some of the pressure off. Give it some thought." Linc whistled to the mare and her ears perked up. "See you later, mama."

A while later, Jed had finished lunch and was walking back to the barn when he noticed his truck headed in his direction. He had given his truck keys to Maggie for the day since he had no place to be other than the barn. Jed stopped and waited for Maggie to park the vehicle.

She slipped out from the behind the wheel wearing a grin he hadn't seen in several days. Surmising it was a good meeting with Tasha, he strode over to greet her.

"Howdy. That look on your face tells me the morning was productive."

She held up her hand and slapped him a high five. "Darn right, it was. Not only did I talk with Tasha, but she already had some ideas on her tablet to show me. I want to keep the color scheme the same since Susie's partial to the old blue, white, and black, but she suggested a layout and an open kitchen concept. I'll run it by Mack too, but I am leaning in that direction. Then"—she bounced on her toes—"the contractor showed up and they're going to start clearing tomorrow, which is earlier than I thought. Tasha consulted with them on the time frame and they're finishing up a job and can start in two weeks." Then her face fell.

He asked, "What's the downside?"

She jammed her hands in her front jacket pockets. "With

the fire being so hot, we have to pour a new foundation and footings, but we'll have a basement to store all the mechanical operations which will give me additional floor space upstairs in the diner."

Jed wanted to reach out and touch her cheek in some attempt to offer comfort, but he held back. "That's good news, right?"

"Winter's closing in. What if they can't get the foundation poured? That means we won't start until spring."

"Is that what the contractor said? Because they have additives to put into the concrete for curing in colder temperatures."

Her face brightened and she lifted her face to look at him. His heart flipped in his chest when he stared into her bright-blue eyes.

"That's good news. I didn't think to ask about it and it's been on my mind the entire drive to the ranch."

She hadn't mentioned the apartment above the diner. "And your living space?"

Waving a hand, she said, "That's the easy part. Same footprint but I'm going to add a second bathroom for Susie adjacent to her bedroom and cut down on the living room to add a little more closet space for us both. Projected move-in date will be next May if all goes according to plan. I need the diner open first, so I'll talk to Annie and Linc about renting the cabin until then." She scuffed the gravel with the toe of her boot. "If they agree, you'll be stuck with the two of us as your neighbors for a while."

His heart soared. Living next to Maggie and Susie wouldn't be a hardship at all. "That will give me plenty of time to teach Susie how to ride; she's a natural in the saddle."

"You're a sweet guy—but like I said last night, don't sacrifice getting your job done to entertain her. She'll adjust to our situation. I hope."

Unsure how to respond since he had already said he had

time to work with her daughter, he gestured toward the barn. "Wanna see the little girl? She's doing great and Annie's trying to come up with a name for her. Maybe you can think of something."

Hooking her arm through his, she said, "Lead the way, and then I'll run up to the house to talk to Annie about extending our residency."

He liked the way her arm felt wrapped around his. "And Susie, don't you have to pick her up from school?"

"No. I bumped into Polly in town. She was going into The Trading Post and said she'd swing by and pick her up since I wanted to get back out here."

"It takes a ranch family to raise kids, I guess." He steered her toward the palomino barn.

"You really think Grace Star Ranch is like a family? I know Annie and Linc would do anything for anyone, but with so many personalities, it just seems like you'd have too many different people to be a cohesive unit."

He was sure it was odd for Maggie to understand what ranch life was like here. He'd worked other ranches before landing at Grace Star Ranch, and this place was different. Annie's grandfather, Pops, heaven rest his soul, had made it easy for people to feel comfortable. "Not all ranch owners are like Pops and Annie. They've never treated anyone like they were *just* an employee. We start as friends with common goals and over time, if the ranch hand stays on, they morph into the family that we've created by choice. Look at what happened to me and Polly. Every one of the cowboys from this ranch and others were searching for us after the kidnapping. No one was going to give up. If they weren't searching, they were backfilling chores to keep things running smoothly."

"I remember." She paused as he slid open the barn door.

"And when I got stepped on by a bull and was in the hospital, not only did Annie show up, but she made sure I had space in the bunk room near the dining hall so I could be close to the action, and she even hired a physical therapist to come out and work with me until I was good as new." He'd never forget how it felt when Annie brought him home from the hospital and set him up making sure that he was comfortable. She had gone beyond what a boss needed to do. Annie took care of him like he was family and that he'd never forget.

"Whoa. I knew you'd gotten hurt, but I never realized how far she went to help you get better. That was above and beyond."

Quietly, he said, "It's what this family does."

Maggie withdrew her arm from his as her cell phone rang. She looked at the screen and frowned. "I'll be right in."

He left her as she walked away from the barn and stood in the middle of the gravel road. Entering the building from the outside, he gave it a moment for his eyes to adjust and then left the door open wide enough so Maggie could slip in without having to wrangle it. He could hear the agitation in her voice but couldn't make out the words. *If she wanted me to know what the call was about, she'd tell me, but by the tone in her voice and the serious expression on her face, it wasn't good news.*

He grabbed a couple of carrots and swung by his horse's stall. "Hey, Tonks." The gelding lumbered over to him and Jed rubbed the length of his nose before offering him a tasty treat. "Want to go riding this afternoon? I thought we'd show Susie what it's like on the trail. You'd be a good boy with Nahla, right?"

The horse snorted and Jed fed him the last carrot. "Then it's a lesson—you, me, Nahla, and Susie for a short ride."

"Can anyone else come along or is this exclusively a riding lesson?" Maggie reached his side and ran her hand the length of Tonks' neck. He leaned into her gentle touch.

"Sure, there's always room for another horse lover on a trail ride. I know it's been a while since you were in a saddle."

She gave him a smile that didn't quite reach her eyes.

Then, she patted Tonks again before saying, "It has. Maybe I could have a very docile mount."

"That I can do, and some of the other horses need exercise. Annie brought some in for the guests and they don't get enough access to the trail. This will work out perfect."

"Then it's settled. Horseback riding for three after three." She paused, "Susie gets home after three and it was my sad attempt at humor."

He laughed and rolled his eyes. "I knew what you meant. I was just tugging your reins."

She gave him a firm punch in his bicep. "Watch out, cowboy. I might just leave you in the dust."

Jed wished he had it in him to ask her on a date and heck —if he had his druthers—she'd be right by his side. And maybe even for the long haul.

15

"Mom, are you coming?" Susie poked her head around the edge of the door. "If you don't hurry, we'll only be riding in the paddock."

Maggie studied her reflection in the narrow mirror hanging on the back of the door. She had dressed carefully for the horseback ride with Jed and Susie doing her best to process the call from Cora Davis, the manager of River Junction Bank. There had been some sizeable withdrawals from her personal savings account, and Cora was letting her know that she was tracking them down. For now, the account was frozen. So, if she needed any cash, Maggie would need to come into the bank and make the transactions personally.

She shook her head. No one had access to the account since Cash left. It had been a joint account, not that he had even contributed to it, but when she was in town tomorrow, she'd have to swing by the bank and straighten the mess out. Just one more thing to deal with.

She grabbed a down-filled vest from the bed and grinned. "I'm ready. Will you be warm enough?"

"Mom." Her tone was filled with exasperation. "I'm not a toddler. I do know how to dress myself."

"I didn't say that. You're my little girl and I—"

"I am sixteen years old, and I stopped being your little girl years ago. So, can we please just go riding and have a good time?"

Before Maggie could answer, Susie stomped out the door, allowing it to slam behind her. Stunned at her daughter's outburst, Maggie followed behind her only to see her sprinting across the road in the direction of the barn. "At least there's something she's excited about." She dropped her chin to her chest. *Just wait until I tell her we're going to stay on the ranch until the diner is rebuilt.* In the distance Jed stood outside. He held up his hand in greeting and she lightly ran down the steps, eager to start the ride.

Jed had three horses saddled and ready to go. Tonks was tethered to a hitching post while the horse Susie sat astride pawed at the ground with a snort. The third horse was a pale-gray color.

"This is Birch. She's gentle and is designated to be one of the horses for guests of Grace Star Dude Ranch."

Jed handed her the reins before cupping his hands to give her a leg up. Inwardly, she groaned; she wasn't a light weight like Susie.

With a twinkle in his eyes, he said, "Don't worry. I've got you."

"On three, I'll swing my leg over." Maggie held on to the saddle horn with the reins resting on the mare's neck. Her other hand was on the cantle, the part that supported her tush.

She stepped into his hand, and he said, "One, two, three."

Seconds later, she sat tall in the saddle, feeling like she'd always been there. Grinning, she pointed to Tonks. "Care to join us?"

In a flash his foot was in the stirrup, and she couldn't help but notice how his jeans hugged his backside as he mounted Tonks. Heat flooded her cheeks, so she looked away and caught Susie staring at her. If she could have said, *oh Mom*, she would have. Instead, Susie looked at the cowboy.

"Which way are we headed, Jed?"

"If it's okay with your mom, I thought we'd ride toward the river. There is an easy path and at this time of day, we shouldn't encounter any wildlife."

"Like bears and mountain lions?" A quiver filled Susie's voice.

"There's nothing to worry about." He touched the side of his jacket. "I've got my sidearm, but most likely we'll see deer. They like to come out this time of day."

Susie tapped the heels of her boots lightly on Nahla's flanks and the horse eased forward, as if understanding where Jed said they were headed. Tonks and Birch walked abreast of each other, and Susie took the lead.

Jed adjusted his hat and made a clicking sound with his tongue for Tonks to pick up the pace slightly. "How was the rest of your day?"

"Stressful." As much as she'd like to talk to him about what had happened earlier, she didn't want Susie to overhear the conversation and give her something else to worry about. "Maybe we can talk later?"

"You know where I live."

She laughed softly. "That I do. What about you? Did you get everything accomplished despite lack of sleep?" Conversation was easy between them, and it made Maggie think back to when she had briefly lived with Cash. Every conversation was laced with lingering anger about her getting pregnant and insisting she was going to have the child. She had never asked him to stay. It was about appearances for him. Leaving a pregnant woman wasn't an option, but leaving the woman who had his daughter was a snap and he never looked back.

"Sleep is overrated." The horses began to canter, keeping pace with Nahla.

Maggie fixed her gaze on Susie. She had a good seat and seemed to be holding her own, gently rolling with the horse's gait. A light breeze teased at her long blond ponytail, and she glanced over her shoulder, Susie's face beaming with happiness. Had she been wrong all these years to not let her ride for fear she'd get the rodeo bug like Cash?

"Nickle for your thoughts?" Jed asked.

"Huh?"

"You might want to loosen your grip, so Birch doesn't get the wrong signals." He nodded to her death grip on the reins.

Instantly, she relaxed her fingers, stretching them out and back into an easy hold. "I went down a rabbit hole. Sorry."

"Something else you want to talk about tonight?" He eased back on the reins to slow Tonks to a walk and whistled for Susie to do the same. He called out, "We're getting close to the river, and we need to turn around in about five minutes."

She adjusted her seat in the saddle and said, "Already? We just got started."

"It'll be dark soon and we can go back a different way to stretch the return trip a bit." He glanced at Maggie. "Is that okay with you?"

She nodded, relieved Susie was now facing forward and wasn't going to argue with him. As far as Maggie was concerned, Jed called the shots out here. "She's comfortable on Nahla. Once we move back to town, I know she's going to want a horse of her own. She'll have grown accustomed to having them around, living out here." She took in the view, awestruck by the mountain range in the distance, the gurgle of the river up ahead, and the wide-open space on either side of the trail—except for the occasional tree that would offer a bit of shade in the summer. It had been years since she felt this carefree. Typically, she'd be prepping for the dinner rush. Not so much this time of year, but there were kids coming in after school, the occasional family going out, or even date night for some couples. She couldn't complain. The diner had provided her and Susie with a comfortable life. Even if it took long hours and a lot of hard work.

"I forgot how spectacular the ranch is this time of year." She inhaled the crisp, fresh air.

"Maybe you've spent so much time working that you don't remember how to enjoy the simple pleasures life has to offer."

She didn't take that as a condemnation of her life; Jed was stating the facts. It wasn't a secret she was always working except for two weeks of the year when she shut down and took Susie on vacation. It was important they had time away from their small town, so they went to places like San Francisco or Dallas. Picking cities gave Susie a glimpse of another way of life and Maggie allowed her daughter to choose their destination.

"Turning around," Susie called out.

Jed grinned. "She's a good kid, you know."

"Thanks."

He gave her a quizzical look. "I can tell you have a lot on your mind. I won't bug you anymore. We can just ride."

Nahla and Susie trotted past them, and Maggie shook off her contemplative state of mind. "No need for silence, but you know a lot about me, and I know almost nothing about you. So, spill all the good and bad details. What is your greatest fear, happiest moment, and wish for the future?"

"Mags, there's not much to tell. What you see is what you get."

"Then start by telling me why you call me Mags. It rolls off your tongue like we've known each other our entire lives."

"It feels like we have." Red crept up his neck to his cheeks. "Sorry. But I like you." The heat seemed to evaporate from his face.

"That's a good thing. I like you, too." But were they on the same unspoken page?

"Anyway, I have parents and a sibling, but we don't see

eye to eye. So, when I turned twenty,-two I packed up my stuff in an old pickup truck and headed to Montana from a ranch in a small town outside Fort Worth. I bounced around for a few years, working at different ranches until I landed here about ten years ago. I didn't intend to stay longer than a couple of years like usual. Then, one day, I was gettin' the itch to pack up and hit the road, and Pops came down to the horse barn. I remember it just like it was yesterday. He asked me if I was about done runnin' away from life."

"Annie's grandfather asked you that? How did he know you had a restless spirit?"

Jed gave her a side-look and said, "The man could read people better than anyone I've ever met. Of course, I said I wasn't runnin' from anything serious, and he said he already knew that. Said I was a good man, he could tell by the way I treated the animals and the other ranch hands. Then he asked me to do us both a favor and stick around for six months longer than I had ever stayed anyplace else and if I was still itchin' to leave, he'd help me find my next gig."

"It doesn't need to be said, but I'm glad you stuck around." Her heart ached for the young man who felt he didn't have a home.

"It was the best decision I've made to date. Now, I have friends who are like a real family to me, a job I love, a good roof over my head, and great neighbors, even if they do tend to bang doors occasionally."

Now it was Maggie's turn for heat to flush her cheeks. "I'll see what I can do to curb that."

"Are you kidding? It makes things a bit livelier around here." He chuckled, "For the record, my favorite food is your huckleberry crumble, and my all-time favorite meal is a stack of silver dollar pancakes dripping with maple syrup and thick-slab bacon."

"That's a lot of favorite foods"—she did air quotes around

favorite foods—"but don't stop there. What's your favorite vacation spot and ice cream?"

"I've never taken a real vacation as an adult—and for ice cream, it's vanilla on top of your crumble."

He gave her a wink and it dawned on her, then. He'd often order the pancakes and bacon at the diner and when she reopened she'd have to make sure to have crumble always on the menu. She could do one better and make one for him just as soon as she could put her hands on some berries. After all, it was the least she could do for him when the only favorite foods he mentioned came from her kitchen.

few days later, Jed was hauling a couple of hay bales into each horse stall when he heard, "Hey, cowboy." It was coming from the paddock area. He placed the bale outside of Bowie's stall and went out a side entrance.

Susie and Maggie were bundled in heavy coats and knitted hats against the chill that had settled over the valley earlier in the day. They leaned over the fence with apples in their outstretched hands.

Maggie gave him a wide smile. "Busy today?"

"Same as usual." He stepped up on the lower rung of the fence next to Maggie. "What brings you ladies down to the paddock?"

Susie leaned forward so she could see Jed around her mom. "I was hoping we could go for a ride. I've been thinking if I get comfortable enough that I could learn barrel racing."

He nodded. Interesting how this idea had taken root. Could it be tied back to her absentee father? Nah. More likley some of her friends were into the rodeo.

"Since we don't know much about it, we thought you

might." Maggie gave him a wide-eyed look as if she was trying to convey another message to him.

"Anyone can learn to race if they're patient. You'd need an instructor and a mount that is quiet, well broken in. I think some new tack would be in order and lots of practice. You won't pick it up overnight, but with some patience and a slow, steady approach, you could."

Maggie's facial expression never changed.

Susie beamed. "Any chance I can take Nahla out today?"

He gave her a steady look, one he hoped would slow her race to the barrels. "She's not suited for that kind of work."

"Oh, I know, but I should get more confident just riding and galloping, don't you think?" She glanced at Maggie. "Please, Jed? I can saddle her up and take care of her after, and I'll just stay in the paddock. Right in plain sight of you and Mom."

"Suz, I'm sure he has work to finish."

This was the first time he'd seen Susie this animated since the last time she rode. "Mags, it's okay. If she really wants to learn taking care of her mount from start to finish, that's good, but it will be under my supervision and if I tell you to redo something for Nahla, you'll do it without a complaint, unless you have a question."

"You bet." She pushed off from the fence and landed on the scrub grass. "Is she in her stall?"

He nodded in the direction of the barn. "She is and you can get started, but before you get on, I'll check the saddle and bridle to make sure you did them correctly."

She held up her hand and slapped him a high five before dashing off to the barn. Maggie watched until she was inside before looking at Jed. "You didn't need to agree."

"Riding is good for her. It's the only time she's really happy out here. I thought it would help you if she had something positive to focus on."

Maggie looked off in the direction of the river, even though they couldn't see it.

The thought of the water slipping over rocks and around bends brought a sense of peace to his soul.

"I don't want her to turn into a female version of Cash."

And there it was. An old fear rearing up like a wild stallion. She had done a good job controlling her thoughts when Susie was around.

He slipped his arm around her shoulders and gave her a gentle hug. "It's not the same thing. From what little I know, he had the rodeo bug from the time he pulled on his first pair of boots. Susie's got a good head on her shoulders. She's not about to go off half-cocked and run around with the rodeo."

"A few months ago, I would have agreed. But now, with all that's happened and our life in an upheaval, she might think it's the perfect time to throw caution to the wind and lasso her future that doesn't include college."

"You're selling her and you short. That kid has a good head on her shoulders and despite the current circumstances, that won't change. Giving her some responsibility with a horse will help in the long run."

"You could be right. But you already brought up a good point about Nahla. I'll need to buy her a horse, tack, and pay for lessons. That's a lot of cash outlay."

He touched her shoulder and lightly placed his finger under her chin and guided her to look at him. "Do you think I would have agreed if I didn't have some kind of an idea what this all would cost and how it might be achieved without causing a pinch to your finances?"

Now he had her full attention.

"I'm listening."

"We'll talk to Tate Dunn. I'm not sure if you've had a chance to get to know him yet. He used to ride the circuit and his sister was a good barrel racer, and he worked with her. I'm sure if you talk to him, Tate will agree to help out and we might even have a suitable mount to get her started. He'll know that, too."

"Then all I'd need to get is the saddle?" She wasn't talking to Jed but more like walking through what her next steps needed to be. "Will you introduce us tomorrow after I get back from taking Susie to school? I don't want her to know in case he says he can't do it. Then, if she gets real serious about it, we can talk about buying her a horse down the road." She gave him a peck on the cheek. "You know, you're pretty good at the parent thing. Why didn't you ever have any kids?"

"Missing one little part of the equation." He arched his brow as his mouth went dry. "The right woman to have some with." And for Jed Steele, the only woman who had ever come close to giving him those kinds of ideas was standing next to him.

"Jed." Susie came out of the barn leading Nahla at a steady pace. "Ready for inspection."

He stepped off the fence and crossed to where the girl and mare had come to a halt. Rubbing the velvety softness of the mare's nose he said, "Are you ready to take Susie out for her next lesson?"

She nickered softly as if she understood the question.

He ran his fingers over the bridle and gave Susie an encouraging smile. "Good job. How did you do with the blanket and saddle?"

"I did it just like you showed me, and I took my time, too. I used the same saddle as before; I hope that's okay."

"Fine." He stopped and crossed his arms over his chest. "Tell me the steps you took."

She draped the reins over her shoulder and held up her index finger. "I brushed her down and checked the underside of the pad, then I placed that on her back, making sure there weren't any bumps. I was gentle when I put the saddle on her." She popped up another finger. "Then I made sure the girth strap was tight in the ring along with the other one."

"The tie strap?" He was impressed so far, but he was not about to let on.

"Right. I made sure the strap was tight and saddle straight. Then, I double-checked to make sure the strap was secured since I don't want that coming loose as we're trotting the length of the paddock." She flashed him a wide grin that warmed her sable-brown eyes.

He checked all aspects of the saddle and said, "Good job. Go ahead and mount, and I'll open the gate for you."

"Thanks a lot. This is so totally cool." Putting her left boot-clad foot in the stirrup, she vaulted into the saddle with the grace of an experienced and confident horsewoman. He glanced at Maggie who lifted one shoulder. In his opinion, this young woman was born to ride.

"Have fun and don't push yourself or Nahla. Work together. That's what a good barrel racer does with her mount. It's teamwork."

She tapped the brim of her cowboy hat and said, "Got it." She pressed her knees into Nahla's side, and they entered the paddock. He secured the gate behind them and watched as Susie and Nahla made their way at a slow walk halfway down the space before breaking into a gentle trot and then canter. They circled the paddock a couple of times at varying rates. Maggie stood quietly beside him.

"She's a natural, just like you said."

He was not surprised at her statement. "To ride yes, I have no comment on barrel racing. People usually start much younger, but that's not to say she can't if she sets her mind to it."

"She blames me, you know."

"For her father taking off?"

"Yeah, in a small way."

"You shouldn't carry that guilt. If Cash had wanted to be a part of her life, he would have. He's the one who should feel guilt, not you."

She glanced his way. It has been an interesting conversation so far and he had the feeling she was about to make it even more so.

"Guilt is a funny thing. Have you given any thought to the burden you've been carrying around about Polly?"

Not being able to help her had eaten at him like a festerin' wound. Maggie had been right; he needed to talk about it and let it go. "I have given what happened a lot of thought, replayed it in my mind over the last few days. Even when I examine every detail, I just can't see what I could have done differently."

She placed her hand on his. "But did you talk to Polly? Does she blame you for what happened?"

"I went up to the greenhouse earlier today and we had a good talk. Basically, she said that I more than likely saved her life by jumping in the way I did. He had to figure out how to dispose of us both and that gave her time to get free and disable him until help arrived."

"And…" Maggie prodded.

"Bottom line, she told me that the guilt I've been wrestling with was a waste of time and she never blamed me for what happened. In fact, she's been carrying a mess of guilt that I got hurt, so we hugged it out and agreed to put it behind us. Permanently."

"Now, that I would have liked to see," she said, her tone teasing Jed. "I do know how to hug, you know, and even more than that."

Her eyes twinkled. "I'm sure you know how to do all kinds of things. Maybe it's time you come out of that shell of yours and ask a woman on a date."

He opened his mouth with a quick comeback, but it died as he locked his eyes on Susie. She was racing down the length of the paddock in their direction and with daylight fading fast, he wasn't sure if she had control over Nahla or if the horse was controlling the situation. In this particular case, he hoped Nahla did.

Just as they were about to crash into the fence, and Susie wasn't pulling up on the reins, Nahla came to a skidding halt. Susie lost her seat and was falling from the horse. Maggie scrambled up and over the top of the fence, dropping to a dead run with Jed right beside her.

Maggie sank to her knees. "Susie, are you okay?"

Sitting up, she grinned. "I'm gonna be a little sore on my backside tomorrow, but the good news is, I got my first fall done with." She looked at Jed and her grin faded.

"Just what were you thinking coming in that fast? Do you know in this light, Nahla could have had a misstep? What if she'd broken a leg?"

Susie scrambled to her feet and looked at the horse, and that is when it hit her. "Jed, I am so sorry. I never thought that anything bad could happen." She grasped the reins and kissed the mare's neck, all the while murmuring how sorry she was.

"Take her back to the barn and cool her down. Don't forget her oats and maybe even an apple." He knew his voice was gruff, but he needed to be stern. These animals were his responsibility and if something had happened to Nahla or Susie, he'd never forgive himself.

"Jed?" Maggie said as Susie led Nahla into the barn. "She made a mistake. Did you need to be so harsh?"

He turned his gaze to her. "Yes."

She opened her mouth, to speak, but looked at his face and her words died. Continuing to stare at him, she finally said, "I'm very sorry."

He turned and strode to the barn.

17

The next morning Maggie knocked on Susie's bedroom door. "Get a move on because before we leave, you're going to find Jed and apologize again." It was quiet on the other side of the door. Dang it, had she overslept? They were going to be late for school. She tapped on the door again and eased it open. The bed was a rumpled pile of blankets, but no Susie.

She stepped back into the hallway and glanced at the bathroom door which was standing open and no sounds were coming from inside the small room. Where the heck was Susie?

Walking back into the kitchen, she noticed Susie's backpack wasn't near the door. Now worry began to sneak in. Grabbing a coat from the peg near the door, Maggie pulled it open and jogged down the front porch steps. Her new SUV was in its parking place so at least Susie hadn't decided to drive herself to town. Looking up and down the gravel road that went deeper into the ranch or lead back to the road, she glanced in the direction of the horse barn. Was it possible her daughter had gotten it in her head to ride this morning?

She crossed the gravel road, her steps filled with a new purpose. Once she reached the barn, she slid back the heavy door and stepped inside. The smell of sweet hay teased her senses and she listened, wondering if she'd figure out where to look first. All she heard was the sound of a rake and shovel scraping against the cement floor. Maggie assumed Zak was cleaning a stall. She was about to turn around when she noticed a familiar-looking backpack propped against a wooden bench. It was Susie's so she had to be in here. She wouldn't have taken Nahla out for a ride without Jed around, would she? Ever since she got the idea to learn how to barrel race, all she had talked about was learning to ride better so she could get her own horse.

Propelled by a rising sense of anger, Maggie hurried deeper into the barn, not looking right or left until she got to Nahla's stall. There she saw Susie shoveling a pile of manure into the wheelbarrow just inside the stall door.

"What are you doing?" Maggie asked.

Susie snapped her head up. "Mom. What does it look like? I'm taking care of Nahla. Since I've been the only person riding her lately, I thought it was the right thing to do to pitch in and help out."

The anger that flared in Maggie immediately was doused. "Does Jed know you're out here?"

With a quick nod, Susie turned her attention back to shoveling. "I asked him if it was okay to pitch in and he said if I wanted to have my own horse, I needed to put in the effort. Like proving I'm capable, not just a kid begging her mom for a horse and then not doing my part."

This was an interesting turn of events, but why hadn't Jed given her a heads-up?

Susie leaned into lifting the shovel and the last bits of hay and manure were cleaned up. "I know that look and can guess what you're thinking."

She quirked a brow. "Really? Do tell."

"You think Jed should have told you that he and I talked and he agreed it was a good idea. In his opinion, taking initiative is the best way to show that I'm ready."

Maggie crossed her arms over her midsection. He had been right, although one day doing chores in the barn didn't make a huge impact, but it was a start. "You should leave yourself enough time to get cleaned up before school. And now we need to leave in ten minutes."

Susie looked down at her jeans. "Yeah, I need to change. There's a good amount of droppings on my clothes. This afternoon, I'll put these back on and finish my chores. Tomorrow, I'll come down earlier, then shower and get ready for school."

"Good idea. Now, how about I go lay out a fresh pair of jeans and socks and you can pick your own shirt when you come up. It will save a minute or two."

Before she knew what was happening, Susie threw her arms around Maggie and hugged her tight. "Thanks, Mom. I never thought you'd be this cool about everything."

It had been a while since her daughter had hugged her with happiness. Maggie had chalked it up to the teen years, but maybe she had needed something more in her life than school, working in the diner, and her friends. Back to the ranch, she'd talk with Jed about a finding a horse for Susie that would be suitable for barrel racing. It was time to loosen the reins a bit and give Susie more leeway with her future— even if the idea of her within one hundred yards of a rodeo as a participant made Maggie break out in a cold sweat. *The last thing I need is for Susie to accidentally bump into Cash. Charming and slick and the man could sell a saddle to a woman who was allergic to horses.*

"Put a wiggle on it and get back to the cabin just as soon as you've put your tools away. And I'll have everything ready for you."

"Thanks, Mom. And a double thanks for not being mad."

Maggie cupped her daughter's cheek and looked into her eyes. Her heart swelled with pride and love for the young woman standing in front of her. "Next time tell me what you're doing. Don't just disappear. I was scared half to death."

A grin appeared on Susie's face. "Momma, we're living in the middle of a ranch. Where the heck could I go? Town's a bazillion miles away and none of my friends are going to get up extra early just to pick me up for school."

"I'll remember that. And next time, I'll check the barn before jumping to worry."

Susie pointed toward the barn door. "Put a wiggle on it, Momma; time's a-wastin' and you don't want me to be late for school."

With a laugh, Maggie left the barn and, as promised, would set out clean clothes and even have the bathroom ready for a quick shower. Susie was wearing the scent of Eau de Nahla.

After dropping Susie at school, Maggie drove to the diner. She winced when she saw the big empty plot of land where the diner used to stand. A couple of guys walked around the burnout site with Tasha Melnick. Putting the car in park and zipping her coat she hurried from across the street. TFlickikng up the collar against the sharp, cold air, she glanced at the sky. She wouldn't be surprised if the first snow wasn't right around the corner but not today. *What would that do to construction?* A heavy storm could grind it to a standstill until spring and that would devastated her bank account.

Tasha held up a hand and waved her over to a desk area, which was really two sawhorses and a rectangle of plywood.

As Maggie drew closer, she saw the pages were blueprints. A smile spread over her face.

"Morning," she said to no one in particular. She was surprised to see Jesse, the foreman for the ranch project, looking over the prints.

"Maggie, I'm glad you're here." Tasha waved her closer to the group. "I'd like to introduce you to Jesse Ryan. He's agreed to oversee the project and today the crew is coming to set the forms for the foundation and the concrete company is coming tomorrow morning."

Jesse grinned at her. "Hi, Maggie."

"Hey, how can you be here *and* at the ranch?"

His grin broadened. "Annie wants your diner to get up and running as soon as possible so she insisted I work for you. I'll oversee the ranch project, but I left Margo, who is amazing at finish work, in charge since we're at that phase." If he noticed her lips thin, he was wise not to mention it. "The concrete will take a little longer to cure in this weather even with accelerators added, but I'm going to set up a temporary office out in back so the guys have a place to get warm and get supplies on order to keep the project moving along. I'll also bring in temporary containers for storage. I can promise there won't be any time wasted since we want to get the frame up and enclosed as quickly as possible. If we can beat the first big storm, the interior work will take the most time, but you should be able to reopen early spring."

"Oh," was all she could think to say. Logically, rebuilding took time, but she hadn't ever really thought about how long it would take even if the projected completion date was May. Silence cloaked around her like heavy wool. She looked up at the workers, Tasha, and Jesse. "What do you need from me to get things going?"

Tasha smiled. "That's the easy part. You step back and let these folks get to work."

Nodding, she said, "What time are you going to get

started in the morning?" Her mind was already turning with how to get hot coffee and snacks for them to eat. After all, the one thing she could do was keep them supplied with muffins, cookies, and plenty of coffee.

"We'll start at seven and quit around three, depending on what we're working on. But feel free to stop by anytime. Just check in with me."

Maggie frowned. She couldn't believe she'd have to get permission to be at her own building.

"It's for safety reasons only, Maggie. I'm going to assume you've never been on an active construction site, and if you're not familiar with what's going on, it can be dangerous."

Glancing at Tasha, who nodded in agreement, she said, "How about I text you when I'm headed over and we'll plan to meet at the trailer?"

"Sounds like a plan. Now, if you ladies don't mind, I'm going to get this crew rolling." He walked away and a sharp whistle broke the air. Maggie guessed that was his way of getting things rolling. She focused her attention on Tasha.

"I can't thank you enough for working so fast on my project."

Tasha withdrew a pair of wool gloves from her jacket and pulled them on. "I love doing this kind of stuff and, to be honest, I hate that this happened to you. Women business owners need to stick together and help each other when we can." Her smile widened. "Besides, I happen to love your waffles."

"You've been to the diner?"

"Every time I go out to the ranch, I've stopped in and tried several items, but your waffles are just like my nana's."

"Thank you. That's nice to hear. When we reopen, waffles are on me." As Maggie talked, a dark-gray dually pickup, with tinted windowa drove slowly past. A shiver raced down her spine. She sucked in a breath, immediately thinking of Cash, but she pushed that thought away. *There was no way*

Cash Gordon would ever set foot in River Junction again. He'd made that crystal clear the day he walked out on her and Susie.

"What's wrong?" Tasha touched her arm. "You look like you saw a ghost."

She glanced at Tasha but couldn't shake an ominous feeling. "I'm just chilled."

18

It was midafternoon when Jed drove through the gate of Stone's Throw Ranch. He was on to talk with Ford Shepard. At one time the man had a knack for the right mount for a specific person. *If anyone could help me find the right horse for Susie, it'd be Ford.*

It had been a while since he'd been over this way. Henry senori stood near the main house. He held up his hand in greeting. Jed slowed the truck and leaned out the open window. "Hey there Henry."

The older hand thrust his hand out and shook Jed's. "It's been a while since you've been over. I suspect they're keeping you busy at GSR?"

"Yes sir. We're the expanding horse enterprise so there's a lot to do."

"Good. Glad to hear things are going well for Annie. She's a great gal."

"That she is. Any chance you could point me in Ford's direction?"

"Head down to the ranch office. He should be doing paperwork, at least that's what he said was the plan for the afternoon."

"Thanks, say hello to Maeve for me."

"Will do. Take care now."

He pulled away and parked outside near a door with the sign OFFICE next to it.

The door burst open and a boy—maybe six years old—came running out and ran straight into Jed. "Hold on there, little dude, where are you going in such a hurry?"

The boy looked up at him. "Going to the house. Dad says I have to do my chores before I can ride my pony."

Nodding solemnly, Jed stepped aside to let the boy pass. "Then, go on now."

The child took off running as fast as his short legs could carry him. He walked into the office and Ford sat behind an enormous wood desk. "Yours?" He nodded in the direction of the door.

"Yes, that's Toby and he likes to see how far he can push me before I'll cave. But when it comes to chores, I never give in. They have to get done before he can take out Dusty, his pony." As if that needed further clarification.

He gestured to the empty chair across the desk. "Have a seat. Coffee?"

Jed shook his head. "No, thanks on the coffee." He sat down. "I hope I'm not wasting your time. I talked with Tate Dunn and he said you're like a matchmaker for horses and people."

He leaned back in the old-style wooden office chair. "He's a good man," and he chuckled, "Now, that's interesting. I've never been called a matchmaker." A thoughtful expression came over his face. "I guess I could see why some might say that. But why do you need my help in finding a horse?"

"It's not for me. You know Maggie Brady?"

He nodded. "Too bad about the diner. But I heard

construction has started, so that's good. Has the sheriff caught the person who's responsible?"

"Not yet, but he will." Jed spoke with a confidence that he believed, but he was also feeling more pessimistic with each passing day. Not that he could ask Tye the status since it wasn't his business, but from what little Maggie had shared, there were no new leads.

"Good. It's a downright shame that some jerk went after Maggie and her daughter. But talking about the fire is not why you came over. How can I help?"

"It's Susie, Maggie's daughter. She's been learning to ride with Tate and is interested in barrel racing but she needs the right horse. We don't have a mount at the ranch that is suitable for a beginner so I was hoping you'd know of a few that Maggie and Susie could check out, see if one would make a good match. We'll board her at GSR."

He gave him a thoughtful look. "If she's new to riding, who's going to teach her to race?"

"You know Tate Dunn; he worked with his sister and is prepared to help Susie."

Ford steepled his fingers and said, "Give me a couple of days and I'd like to go with them to meet the horses. I can guide Susie to the best mount for her."

Jed grinned. "Like a matchmaker." He stood and extended his hand. Giving him a hearty shake, he said, "Thanks for your help. And Ford, good to see that you and Toby have settled in. I know you haven't had it easy. Being a single parent and all."

"Thanks. Sharon hasn't even bothered to see Toby since we moved here. She barely calls, and when she does, it just gets him riled up so I guess for now it's better this way. He's got my parents along with Renee and Hank. He loves hanging out at the orchard too. It's a far cry from when we were living in Tennessee where we had no family around. And he's made friends at school—so life has definitely improved for us both since Hank talked me into moving back."

"It's good to have family around." He pulled open the office door. "I'll look forward to hearing from you."

"Happy to help—and you say Susie's comfortable on a horse?"

Jed paused in the doorway. "Not that I'd say this to Maggie, but the girl inherited something from her father. He's on the rodeo circuit and you'd swear Susie had been on horses her entire life. I've never seen anyone who was born to be in the saddle like that girl."

"Good to know. It helps me narrow things down."

"Thanks again, Ford." Jed crossed to his truck and got in. Just mentioning how good it was to have family around was like a gut punch. After his parents disowned him for making the decision to be a ranch hand instead of going into the family grocery store business, he'd never looked back. The only connection he had to his parents was the occasional walk into a Big Sky Market, which was a part of the chain of food stores his family owned in the western half of the country. He gripped the steering wheel, remembering their last argument when his father announced since he had no desire to learn the ropes, they would turn everything over to his younger sister, Julie. That had been sixteen years ago, and he'd never looked back. He pushed the rest of the memories away and started the truck. He had better things to do than dwell on what would never change.

The barn door slammed with a thud. Jed looking up from the feed order. He smiled knew it was Susie by the humming of a popular tune. It was something Maggie did, except they were show tunes—it sweet that she took after her mom. He swiveled in the chair, watching the door, hoping she'd pop into his office like she had done the last couple of days. The soft sounds of her voice were for words just for Nahla. A bonded pair. *It was a shame Nahla wouldn't make a good barrel racing horse; she had no training.* Besides, they needed a gentle mount in the stables for the dude ranch guests.

Since Susie didn't come to him, Jed pushed back from the desk to search her out. He adjusted his cowboy hat on his head on the way out of the office.

Maggie walked into the barn. When her eyes locked on his an his heart quickened and his mouth went dry. *At some point, I'm gonna to need to cowboy up and ask the woman out on a proper date.*

"Mags, how're things going in town?"

She did a little jig in the middle of the wide aisle and grinned. "It's pretty darn exciting. Containers have been delivered along with the supplies to fill them up; the office trailer is on-site, and temporary electric and water are hooked up. The foundation is ready for them to start framing, so, all in all, we're moving at the speed of light."

"Any news from the sheriff?"

She shook her head and stood next to him. Sticking her hands in her coat pockets, she withdrew a pair of gloves and put them on. "Not yet, but I put up security cameras every-where and if anyone goes onto the jobsite after three when the crew is done, I'll get an alert. All I need to do is call the sher-iff's office and they'll get someone right over there. So, I'm not worried about a repeat performance."

"That's great news." He gave her a one-armed hug and breathed in what smelled like cinnamon and sugar. "What have you been up to today?"

"Baking. Thanksgiving is only two weeks away, so I've been making coffee cakes and muffins and freezing them for delivery the week of the holiday."

"That explains the spices."

She laughed, "Hazard of the job as a baker."

"I'm glad I found you here. I wanted to talk to you about something." She glanced at Nahla's stall. "Can you spare a few minutes for a quick walk?"

He wanted to say anything for her, but instead, he said, "Sure. I'll tell Susie we'll be outside in case she needs—oh, she doesn't need me she's wrapped up in crooning with her favorite four-legged soul."

Maggie smiled as he shortened his stride and fell in step beside her. Holding the door as they exited the building, he pointed to a bench that was in the afternoon sun. "How about we sit over there, the bench is shielded from the breeze by the barn."

He stared across the paddock giving her time to gather her thoughts.

"I wanted to talk about Susie and barrel racing. Do you think she's ready for something like that? I mean, she's never had much interest in riding until we moved out here."

Jed let his thoughts settle, trying to determine how to answer without causing her to get upset by his honest opinion. But they were friends, and he wanted to be up front with her.

"Mags, she's a natural. It's like she was born in a saddle."

Slumping her shoulders, she said, "That's not exactly what I wanted to hear. She has more of him in her than I thought. This is a case of nature, not nurture."

He didn't hesitate and took her gloved hand in his, applying gentle pressure in a half-hearted attempt to reassure her—of what he didn't know, for sure. That someday she wouldn't announce she was leaving town to ride the circuit? That she didn't have something from Cash in her DNA?

"This has come out of the blue. Susie never mentioned anything about barrel racing. Riding, sure. She was always talking about a horse."

Jed continued to hold her hand, savoring the warmth

under his calloused fingertips through the wool glove. "I talked with Ford Shepard today."

She lifted her face, her eyes meeting his. He could see her wary look. "About?"

She must know of Ford's reputation, so there was no sense dancing around the watering trough. "I wanted to see if he could find an experienced barrel racer for Susie. He knows she's new to all of it, but he's the best—Maggie, and if she's determined to do this, Tate has agreed to work with her. He'll give her the best chance to succeed."

"What if I don't want her to be good?" She slapped her hand over her mouth and her eyes widened. "I didn't mean that."

"I know you didn't. You're scared the past will repeat itself and she'll leave here, and your dreams for her to experience college will be like tumbleweed. But you have to let Susie find her own path. She needs to live life with your support and no regrets. And by working with, and not against her, you won't alienate her. People need to follow their dreams, and they'll either fall flat on their face or find happiness and maybe even success. Isn't that what you want for your daughter?"

Maggie gave him an assessing look. "Is that what happened to you? Your family didn't support your dream?"

His gut twisted. "We're not talking about me, right now. That's a story that is best forgotten. But yes, in a nutshell, my parents disowned me because I didn't do what they wanted and I haven't seen them in years. I don't want that to happen to you and Susie."

She leaned closer and placed a lingering kiss on his cheek. "I'm glad you followed your heart and you're sitting with me right now, helping me avoid making a terrible mistake."

Jed's heart was like a jackhammer in his chest. He wanted to fold Maggie in his arms and never let go. If for no other reason than she made him feel like the choices he had made in his life were worthwhile and brought him to be in this space and time with her. "That's what friends are for, Maggie."

Her brows knitted together, and she pulled away from him. *What did I say that was wrong?*

"Let me know when Ford calls and if you don't mind, would you go with us to look at the horse? Since I've never bought one before, I want to make sure I'm doing this correctly."

She didn't try to hide the sadness in her eyes. He was sure it was because she had agreed to let Susie do the one thing that scared her the most.

"You can always count on me."

She stood up. "Tell Susie dinner will be ready in an hour."

Since Maggie hadn't extended the invitation to him, Jed said, "Sure, I'll let her know." He stayed on the bench an ache in the middle of his chest as he watched her walk away.

19

After dinner Maggie checked her bank account on line. Cora had told her the withdrawals were still under investigation but now she did a triple take. There was two hundred and fifty thousand dollars as a new deposit from earlier today and she had no idea where it had come from. It was obviously a mistake and she had to wait until the bank was open in the morning before calling to have them reverse it out. It was nice to see a healthy balance. Just for a moment, she dreamed of what it would be like to have that kind of money just sitting around, gathering a tiny bit of interest.

Susie came out of the bathroom, bundled up in a thick bathrobe and towel-drying her long hair. "What are you looking at?" She stopped at the thermostat and inched it up. "It's cold in here, so I just put the heat on sixty-eight, okay?"

"That sounds good. I was paying some bills." She closed the laptop and patted the table where Susie had been sitting at dinner. "Take a seat. I'd like to talk to you for a minute."

As she slid into the chair, she gave Maggie a look that asked, *Am I in trouble?*

Maggie placed a reassuring hand on Susie's. "Don't worry,

its nothing bad. I just wanted to talk about something. Well, a couple of somethings actually."

"All right."

Waiting half a second, she gave Susie a wide smile. "I was talking with Jed earlier and Tate has agreed to work with you as you learn barrel racing."

"Yeah, I bumped into Tate, and he said the same thing." She frowned. "But there isn't a horse on the ranch I can ride while I'm learning."

"Well, that's the second thing I wanted to talk to you about. Jed spoke to a friend of his, Ford Shepard, who has agreed to look for a horse. Once he finds a couple that he thinks are suitable, we'll take a look and get the horse that is perfect for you."

Susie's eyes widened, and her words came out in a rush. "Do you mean I'll have my own horse? But what about the cost and where will we keep it after we move back to town?"

"I've already talked with Annie, and you can board your horse right here which is perfect since we'll more than likely be living at the ranch until April or May." Maggie waited for her to get all pouty again about not being in town with her friends, but in a surprise twist her daughter got up and hugged her tight. *That's been a while.*

"You mean it? After all this time, my dream of owning a horse will be a reality?"

Maggie couldn't contain her smile. "Yes, but the care of the horse will reside with you—water, feeding, exercise, mucking the stall, and you'll need to get a part-time job to help offset the tack that needs to be purchased."

"This is so, so great. Wait until I tell…" Her words trailed off and she hugged Maggie again. "Thanks, Mom. You're the best!" She hurried from the kitchen and her bedroom door closed with a thud.

Maggie could only guess she wanted to call her girlfriends right away and tell them everything. It had been a long time since Susie had actually been excited about something. Teenage girls were tough, and she often wondered how her own mother had survived the years between being the best mommy in the world to the dumbest. But eventually, like all women, daughters came back around to loving and respecting their moms. It was just a matter of time.

Two days later, Maggie was in the ranch kitchen baking under the watchful eye of Quinn. Even though they had arranged specific times for Maggie to bake, he always seemed to be hovering in the background. She wasn't sure if he was afraid she wouldn't clean up after herself or maybe he was waiting for the inevitable tasting opportunity. Either way, it was satisfying just to be working and making money.

Her cell rang and it was Cora Davis from the bank. She was hoping this would answer the question about the money in her account.

She wiped her flour-covered hands on a towel she had tossed onto the worktable. "Hi, Cora." The women exchanged pleasantries even though Maggie was anxious to hear that the money had been returned to the rightful owner.

"Well, Maggie, I know your curious about that sizeable deposit in your account and lucky for you, it *is* your money."

She slumped to a stool next to the table. "Cora, I don't have that kind of money, nor does anyone I know except Annie Grace. And I'm certain she wouldn't make a deposit into my account."

"It wasn't Annie. Apparently, you have an anonymous benefactor out there who wants to remain that way. But it is legitimate with no strings or funny business attached."

"That's not possible." She felt as if all the air had whooshed from her lungs. "Do you know and just can't tell me?"

"All I know for certain is the money is legitimate. It seems someone out there thinks you have a big heart and after helping others, it was time someone helped you."

"How did you learn that?"

Cora laughed softly. "Leave it to you to keep asking questions. We were able to trace the deposit back to a lawyer's office, and they have assured me there is nothing to worry about. But if it would make you feel better, I could have you talk with someone to put the money in a separate investment account just in case."

She nodded and then said, "Yes. I'm not comfortable until I know who was behind the deposit and why. For now, I think it should be held separately. I would appreciate it if you could email me a person I can talk with."

"You'll have a couple of names by the morning. I need to make a few preliminary calls just to pave the way."

"Thanks, Cora—and I appreciate your help." She rubbed a hand over her eyes. "Are you sure this is real?"

"In my entire banking career, I've never heard of anyone doing this, but I'm sure. Take in the kindness of strangers and, for the record, you've been a good friend to many people over the years and now it's come back to you."

After Maggie hung up the phone, she sat looking at the wall, unsure what she should do next.

A man's cough drew her attention, pulling her out of her thoughts.

She looked over at Quinn.

He asked, "Everything okay over there?"

Shaking her head, she stood up. The pies wouldn't bake themselves and no matter how much money she had in her checking account, she needed to fulfill her customers' orders. "You wouldn't believe me if I told you."

"Does it have anything to do with Susie?"

Slowly, Maggie turned and tipped her head. "No. Why?"

"Nothing, I just heard her talking on her cell yesterday

when she thought no one was around. It sounded like she was making plans for a weekend someplace."

She could feel her face scrunch up and quickly relaxed it to smooth away the telltale signs of concern. "I'm sure she was talking to one of her school friends. She's been having a hard time being on the ranch and away from town."

He gave her a rare smile. "You're probably right. Just do me a favor and don't mention that I said anything. I don't want her to think everyone around here is poking our noses into her private business."

"I'll talk to her, but I won't say where I heard it. Thanks for the heads-up." She turned back to the bowl of berries on the worktable folding sugar and spices into the mix. The practiced motions or prepping the the pies for the oven steadied her mind. *Why hadn't Susie mentioned to me she wanted to hang out with her friends.* She slipped the pies in the oven and put the bowl in the sink. Looking out the tiny window over the ranch she nodded, *they'd sort it out after dinner.* Maybe it was good idea she had fun with her friends before a horse claimed every free moment she had.

Her cell rang again and this time the number wasn't familiar to her at all. She had too much work to do to talk with a telemarketer so she let it go to voicemail. Most of the time they didn't bother to leave a message, anyway.

The rest of the afternoon was spent baking pies and sweet breads for her clients. As she was cleaning up, she called to Quinn. "Chef, are you interested in anything for the ranch hands for supper?"

The swinging door between the two rooms opened and he stepped partway into the kitchen. "Are you talking to me?"

She gave him a saucy wink. "Just trying to live up to my end of our bargain. Take your pick of anything on the cooling racks."

He came closer to the table and leaned over, inhaling deeply the sweet smells of baked goods. "How about I take one of the pumpkin spice cakes, a couple of pies, and four breads. Mix it up for the hands. That will go good with the stew and chili I have planned for tonight."

Maggie picked up the items and carried them out to the buffet and then sliced everything to make it easy for anyone who might want a piece or two. Looking around the spacious room, she closed her eyes counting her blessings. *This ranch, these people, and Susie. Life couldn't get much better than what it is at this very moment.* When she opened them, Jed walked through the door, and she smiled. "Hey, cowboy."

2O

"**H**ey, yourself." Jed strode forward, his steps making short work of the distance between them. "Can I help?"

The moment he walked into the dining hall and laid eyes on Maggie holding two pies, his heart melted. This ranch suited her perfectly and the fact she won Quinn over was a miracle in itself. So far, the only people that man seemed to like were Polly and Annie Grace.

She bobbed her head in the direction of the kitchen. "Ask Quinn what else needs to come out and I can get it all arranged before heading back to my place."

Maggie didn't have to ask him twice for help. *He'd walk from here to the mountain range and back again, without boots, if I asked him.* And this cowboy never walked the ranch without wearing his broken-in Justins. He paused at the swinging door and, swallowing hard, he said, "Um, Maggie, can I talk to you for a minute?"

She flashed him a wide smile, the one that always made his heart flip, and it dissolved in an instant. "Watch out."

The door opened and smacked him on the back, knocking his hat to the floor.

She rushed to pick it up and hand it to him, the moment broken. "Are you okay?"

Quinn said, "Sorry, Jed. I didn't know you were holdin' up the doorway." He chuckled as he went back into the kitchen.

"Thanks." He adjusted his hat, hoping his face wasn't red with embarrassment. "I'll be right back."

"You wanted to talk to me?" The space between her eyebrows wrinkled.

Instead, he pushed the door open and said, "It can wait." The door swung shut and he walked straight to the table overflowing with baked goods.

"You all right?" Quinn asked.

"Never better." His words sounded more like a growl. He had the chance to ask Maggie on a date, and he blew it like he was back in high school.

"If you want my advice…"

Jed looked Quinn's way and hoped the expression on his face would stop Quinn from continuing, but apparently, he wasn't easily dissuaded.

He walked across the room. "Go back out there and ask her. I'm pretty sure she's interested by the way her eyes follow you every time you're in the room. And, before you say it's because you saved her and Susie from the fire, I call bull. We all know you've had a thing for her. Heck, when Polly was in trouble, who did Linc ask to speak to Maggie about newcomers in town?" He gave Jed a poke in the center of his chest. "You. And you know why? Because it's not a secret that you're carrying a torch for the woman."

Jed snorted. "Who says *torch* anymore?"

He shrugged one shoulder. "Me." He clapped Jed on the back. "Just think about it." He pointed to the left side of the table. "Those need to go out front."

Jed walked out the door, backside first. *Torch.* He liked Maggie, yes, but it wasn't as if he was considering dating anyone else. *Right, she's the only woman who's captured your interest since you rolled into town.*

"Let me take a couple of these, and we can finish setting up." Maggie took a plate of sliced bread from his hand and a dome-covered cake platter.

He stuttered, "Um. Sure." *Smooth...*

*J*ed helped Maggie store all the orders in the large walk-in freezer and she pulled her coat on as they walked back into the dining room. She gave the dessert table one final look before giving him a flirty wink. "Care to walk me home since we're headed in the same general direction?"

He held open the door and she walked in front of him. She smelled liked ginger and vanilla, probably from all the baking she had done. "When do you start delivering?"

"Monday. It's hard to believe Thanksgiving is Thursday." She pulled her coat closed. "What are you doing for the holiday?"

Jed stuck his hands in his jacket pockets to avoid the urge to take Maggie's hand. "Quinn makes an amazing spread for everyone. Annie and Linc will come down with Mary and Daphne, and there will be a fire going all day in the dining hall. The hands filter in and out from breakfast until well after dark, munching on the never-ending platters. Holidays around the ranch are always food and people focused. You and Susie should join us." He glanced her way. "Unless you have other plans."

"I've always cooked for the two of us, but I can't see how a turkey is going to fit in that tiny oven in the cabin."

He laughed. "It won't. I'll bet Quinn wouldn't say no to an extra pair of hands in the kitchen. I volunteer to peel potatoes and carrots. I'm not much of a cook, but that I can do. Mary tends to be the head chef that day, bossing everyone around, including Quinn."

"That sweet lady wouldn't boss—oh, wait, what am I saying? Mary has always been in charge of us all. And Quinn's okay with it."

As they drew closer to the cabins, Jed's stride grew shorter. If he could have slowed time he would have, just to have a few more moments with her. "I think he looks at Mary like an honorary grandmother as we all do."

They had reached the bottom of the porch steps to Maggie's cabin. Inside, all the lights were on, throwing a soft glow over the porch.

"And here we are." He nodded toward the house. "Tell Susie I said thanks for her hard work today in the barn."

"I wish I had realized how devoted she was to horses long ago." She glanced at the cabin. "Despite my concern about the rodeo, I have faith in her and I need to remind myself she's not her father. She won't bail on her responsibilities."

He dropped his voice. "She's her mother's daughter."

Maggie licked her lips and gazed into Jed's eyes. So often, hers were lit with laughter, but now there was a new intensity in her eyes. His heart pounded, each beat slowing his breath. He wanted to slip his arm around her waist and hold her close, so close she could feel his heart galloping. Just one step was all he needed to take.

She tipped her head to one side. "Will you do something for me?"

He nodded. "Sure. What are friends for?" His mouth went dry at the word friends.

"Kiss me." It wasn't a question but a request.

His eyes widened, and he drawled. "You want me to kiss you?"

"Yes." The word came out as a soft caress.

He took two steps closer, and his lips brushed her cheek.

"No, not like that." Her voice trembled. She tipped her head back and offered him her mouth.

Jed stepped forward, closing the distance between them with one step until only a breath separated them. His heart pounded in his chest, but all he wanted was to…

He pressed his mouth to hers, tentative at first, almost hesitant until it deepened to a slow, mind-bending kiss. He moaned softly—or was that her? The world fell away as she stepped into him and slid her arms around his waist, and he did the same, crushing her to his chest. There it was, his answer; this was not one-sided.

How long they were in each other's arms wasn't lost on Jed. He could stay right where they were forever. She pulled back and gave him a sweet and tender smile that made his heart flip.

"About time you decided to put your mouth where my heart has been, cowboy."

He kissed her again. This time it was tender and passionate, filled with all the longing his heart had held in check. There would be time for their feelings to rise to the surface. For now, this kiss was near perfection.

A loud thump and muttered curse words reached his ears. "Guess Susie needs you." He relaxed his arms, knowing she had to go inside but not quite ready to let her go. "Would you have dinner with me tomorrow night? We can go into Bozeman if you want or stay in River Junction. Your choice."

She tipped her head and looked deep into his eyes. "I know it's cold out, but what if we took a picnic someplace, built a fire, and sat under the stars."

"You'd rather sit outside than get dressed up and let someone wait on you?" She was a rare woman.

"For our first date, I'd like it to be just the two of us. But if you'd rather, we can put this idea on hold."

He cupped her cheek. "A picnic it is. But I'll take care of

everything. You just plan on dressing warm. We can leave around four."

Hugging him tight she whispered, "I wish it was tomorrow at three fifty-nine."

He felt the same way, but he had a lot to do to make it the most romantic night of her life. "Me too."

She stood on tiptoes and pecked his lips one last time before she slipped from his arms. "See you in the morning?"

"You kinda can't escape me." He pointed to his porch. "Being neighbors and all."

Giving him a thoughtful look, she walked up the steps before turning to him. "The fire was the lowest point in my life, but it has also opened my eyes. In these last few weeks, I've seen another side of you and I really like what I see; I like the entire package."

Using his index finger, he pushed back the brim of his hat and grinned. "Oh, so it wasn't until you lived next door that you saw my charms?"

"I never said you weren't charming," she quipped. "But there is so much more to you than you let people see." She touched the corner of her eye and then pointed her finger at him. "I see the real you, Jed Steele."

His heart flipped in his chest. If she saw the real person now and wasn't put off by his quiet nature, that was a good thing for both of them. "Maybe it's you who brings out new sides to me." He ached to sweep her into his arms, spin her around, and confess the truth he had kept secret for a very long time. But not with her daughter mere feet away. He forced the impulse down with a few slow deep breaths. *There will be plenty of time—time for whatever was between them to take root and grow. All I have to do is wait.*

"Good night, Jed."

"Night, Mags. Sleep well." He watched as she stepped over the threshold and closed the door. He couldn't contain the grin that now split his cheeks. Changing direction from his cabin, he headed back to the dining hall in search of Quinn. He wondered what it would take to bribe the best chef in River Junction to create a mouthwatering picnic for him and Maggie. There was one thing he knew about his friend: he might appear to be a grouch, but when it came to others and the pursuit of romance, he loved playing Cupid. And the next person he needed to talk with was Annie. There was a romantic spot over near her parents' old house—complete with a firepit and endless views down the valley and the mountain range. The stars over Montana would shine bright from that vantage point. Jed rubbed his hands together, looking forward to an evening with Maggie, and he would do his best to make it a night to remember.

$\mathcal{M}$aggie pressed her back against the cabin door and ran her fingertip over her lower lip where Jed's kiss lingered. *What would it be like to spend the rest of the night in his arms, kissing him?* Instead, she closed her eyes, picturing herself lying in his arms in front of a fire, under the canopy of stars.

"Mom, you look weird. Do you have a headache or something? If you're tired, I can fix dinner."

She straightened up and the books Susie had spread out around her on the leather-covered sofa. Giving her daughter a warm smile, she said, "Just a little tired. And thank you for the offer, but I have dinner made. I just need to slide the casserole in the oven."

"Cool. I'm going to finish my homework, and then I thought we could look online for saddles and stuff I'll need for when we buy my horse."

"That sounds like a great idea. I'll be right back." She went in the kitchen and placed the chicken casserole in a cold oven as she decided to broach the subject of Thanksgiving. Hopefully, Susie would want to attend what sounded like a bit of a celebration with everyone on the ranch.

When she returned to the living area, she sat in a chair across from her daughter. "Thanksgiving is next week, and I was talking to Jed. It sounds like it's a big deal around here with people helping Quinn out in the kitchen and they have dinner together. What would you think about joining everyone?"

Susie didn't look up. "Sure, that sounds fine. But I've made some plans for the weekend with a bunch of kids from school. I think we're having a sleepover at someone's house Friday night into Saturday."

"That sounds like fun. But I'll need to know where you'll be spending the night so don't forget to share that little detail." She got up. "I'm going to take a shower before dinner." Dropping a kiss on top of Susie's head as she was leaving the room, she noticed a chat window was open on her laptop. "Who are you talking to?"

She closed the laptop screen and looked up, annoyed like Maggie had been snooping in her diary or something. "Mom, a little privacy, please. I didn't grill you about you smooching with Jed before."

Maggie felt her cheeks flush with heat. "You saw us?"

"Plu-eeze. You were standing right outside the cabin; it was hard to miss."

"It was just a kiss."

Susie scooched to the edge of the sofa and studied her mom, a grin sliding across her face. "One that kicked the temperature in here up ten degrees."

Maggie wasn't sure if she liked that description of her and Jed. *Maybe I should explain a little more so thatshe didn't get the wrong impression.* After all, she hadn't dated since Cash left and this was new territory for them. "I like Jed and—in fact— we have a date tomorrow night."

"That's great, Mom. I like Jed. He's a stand-up guy, and I think he's liked you for a while. I saw the way he looked at you when he came into the diner. And to be honest, it doesn't hurt that he's smokin' hot."

"Susie." Her daughter was right, but *she shouldn't be looking at a man old enough to be her father and noticing he was hot.*

"Relax, Mom. I'm just saying those smoldering gray eyes would be enough to turn the head of any woman your age. I'm glad they finally turned yours. Nothing inappropriate here. I like guys my age. I'm looking out for you, and when I'm off living my own life, it's good to know that you'll have Jed around to keep you company."

"We have a few more years before that happens. You need to finish high school and then college. Then you can step out into the world."

Susie sat back on the sofa. "I'm going to wrap up my homework."

Why had she effectively ended the conversation? Typically, she liked talking about ideas for college. *Well, a lots happened over the last few weeks, and we've been looking at the future through a different lens.* "I'm going to shower. Would you set the table?"

"Sure, no prob." Her laptop was open again and she focused on the screen.

Maggie went down the hall and glanced back over her shoulder as she heard the keys clicking on Susie's laptop. She must be chatting with her friends about the holiday break from school. "Have fun making plans for next weekend."

*T*he next morning, after dropping Susie at school, Maggie drove to the diner. *Well, what would be the diner again.* It seemed like every day progress was made and since the framing was complete, with any luck she might be able to reopen sooner than the spring, but she had kept that secret wish to herself. She parked in her usual spot across the street, grabbed her gloves, and secured her scarf around her neck as the temperature hovered near freezing. Thinking the picnic idea for that night hadn't been one of her best, given the forecast for a cold day, she decided to stop by and see Jed to change their plans. No sense in freezing to death on their first date.

She waited to cross the road as a Cadillac SUV crept down the street. It had Montana plates but it wasn't a vehicle she had seen in town. Probably an out-of-towner on their way to someplace else. When it passed, she crossed the street. She could feel her smile growing as she waved to Jesse. "Hey," she called out. Stopping, she dashed back across the street to get the boxes of muffins she baked last night for the crew.

She opened the back and grabbed the three boxes and flicked the hatch closed. Jesse waited for her on the sidewalk.

"Morning, Maggie. You're going to spoil the crew. Every time we start a new job, they will think they'll get sweets."

"Jesse, this is nothing. I want them to know I appreciate each person out here and it's the least I can do."

He took the boxes from her. "Come on into the trailer and we can talk about what's next for the project. I think you're going to be pleased."

She looked around, awed by the men walking on what was the structure for the second floor. She could see where windows would be placed and there were large beams swinging in the air from a crane. "What are those?"

"Roof joists. We want to get them completed today so tomorrow we can start getting plywood on and get this building buttoned up before the first snow." He held open the door to the makeshift office.

When she stepped inside, the warmth and the aroma of coffee perking in the large coffee urn greeted her.

"Thanks again for the goodies. It's definitely a perk for the crew." He nodded. "Including the never-ending supply of coffee."

"It's cold out there." She crossed the small space to where

the plans for her diner were laid out. "What else should I be doing to help?"

"If you know of any sunshine spells, that would be good." He grinned. "Seriously, nothing. We've got the best crew in Montana, and everyone is working hard, racing Mother Nature."

"What happens if you don't get the sides and roof on before it snows?" A tingle of worry washed over her. She hoped he wouldn't say the project would be shut down until it thawed. Did that happen around here? She had never taken notice of construction projects. She was usually too busy with the diner to venture out.

"Then, we shovel snow and get back to work. It just slows things down." He gave her a reassuring smile. "We've done this before. This project isn't the first or last time we'll have to deal with weather issues."

A sharp rap on the trailer door drew Jesse's attention. He pushed it open, and a man stood on the other side. *That must be an inspector of some kind.* She focused her attention on the plans and let Jesse handle it.

"Can I help you?" Jesse asked.

"I'm here to speak with Ms. Brady."

She turned. "I'm Maggie Brady. How can I help you?" The man looked vaguely familiar, but she couldn't place where she might have seen him.

Jesse asked him to come inside.

The stranger was of slight build, but tall. His steel-gray hair was neatly trimmed and his brown eyes were laser-focused on her. It was easy to see he wore his wealth. His suit jacket was tailored, fitting him perfectly with his pressed jeans and an alligator belt, right down to the tips of his alligator boots. The only reason she even knew they were alligator was because Cash had a pair and made sure she knew how much they had cost. Not that he ever helped with child support for Susie. But that was the past. This stranger was standing in front of her now, oozing money.

He held out his hand. "I'm Montgomery Johnson. But my friends call me Monty."

She shook his hand. "It's a pleasure to meet you, Mr. Johnson."

"Monty, please." He flashed her a bright white smile, and with one front tooth slightly overlapping the other, it made him appear less than perfect.

Maggie said, "How can I help you?"

"You already have."

She narrowed her eyes and glanced at Jesse who shrugged his shoulders. "I'm not sure I understand. You may have me confused with someone else. I own, well, owned a diner until we had a fire." She pointed out the window. "We're in the process of rebuilding."

"I've eaten in your restaurant, and you have the best chicken fried steak I've ever had." He wiggled his brows. "Ring any bells yet?"

Slowly, she shook her head. "No, I'm sorry but I don't remember you." *What did this man want?*

"Do you have children, Maggie?"

"A daughter." She pointed to the coffee urn. "Would you like a cup?"

Jesse quickly filled three cups, and Maggie was relieved he wasn't going to leave her alone with Mr. Johnson.

"I have four children." He smiled his thanks to Jesse as he took a cup.

Maggie took one and sat in one of the hardback chairs, and Mr. Johnson sat across from her with Jesse on the other side of the desk.

She crossed her legs and waited. *I'm not about to share more details of Susie with a stranger.*

"As I was saying, I have four children who have grown up

with every possible luxury, and I'm sorry to say they're not the nicest of people. They're not bad; they just tend to be on the selfish side of the spectrum. I decided to teach them a lesson about human kindness. First, I cut off access to their bank accounts and had them live on their paychecks from their actual jobs. But that still didn't make a dent in their ways. So then, I decided to show them people who weren't as fortunate in life as they were who actually lived good, caring lives."

"Mr. Johnson, I'm not sure where you're going with this. If you're looking for me to donate to a cause, I can write you a check. I don't have a lot to give, but I'm happy to help."

"It's Monty, please, and no, I'm not here looking to solicit donations for anything. I'm here because of your kindness."

Now, she was thoroughly confused.

"You really don't know who I am, do you." His voice was gentle, and he said, "Take a closer look." He pulled a ragged old black knit hat from his cashmere coat pocket and put it on. "Now?"

Her hand flew to her mouth. She said, "You're the homeless man I offered a job to in exchange for meals and you got so mad at me."

Monty chuckled. "As you can see, I'm not homeless, but yes, you were kind enough to feed me and offer me a job to help me get back on my feet and you said that River Junction was a great place to live." His eyes twinkled. "And yes, those were your exact words."

She was speechless. She looked at Jesse who looked at Monty and then back to her. He seemed to be at a loss too.

"I'm glad you're not really homeless with winter coming." She cringed. That had been a dumb thing to say. "But I don't understand, what did this teach your kids and why did you get angry with me?"

He grinned. "I'm sorry I yelled at you, I was so overcome with joy that a random stranger would actually help a homeless person down on his luck. It was that or my eyes would have leaked. And now that same man is happy to repeat the kindness. I want to help you rebuild your diner faster so I'm prepared to add to the crew." He looked at Jesse. "That's if you're willing to bring on some more people."

He gave a nod in Maggie's direction. "She's the boss."

Monty's gaze swiveled to Maggie. "What do you say? Let me give you a hand up like you did for me."

Suddenly, all the pieces clicked. The money in her account. She knew where it had come from. "It was you."

He smiled when he realized she had figured it all out. "No strings, Maggie. You helped me teach my kids that it is better to help others than expect to be handed life on a silver platter. It is a debt I can never repay to you."

She stood up. "Thank you, Monty. I accept your offer to add to the crew. With the diner being closed, it's caused a hole in this town that needs to be filled." Maggie knew of the families around town that counted on her specially priced, *well free*, dinner menu at the end of each month when some folks were trying to stretch food budgets. She called it Soup and Slices night. If accepting his help would help her help others, then she would find a way to repay him once she had reopened. "And anytime you want a chicken fried steak, it's on the house."

22

*J*ed came back from Annie's parents' place just down the road from the ranch and drove to the dining hall. Quinn had been a good sport and agreed to fill a basket with picnic fare. Jed didn't care what it was since anything the chef made was one hundred times better than anything he could whip up.

Despite what had happened on the property, being held at gunpoint and thinking his life was going to end, he knew it had the best overlook for the picnic along with a firepit and a small wooden lean-to nearby that he had decked out with cushions and wool blankets. Well, until Annie showed up and finished decorating with some pillows, a couple of small tables, and a rug to cover the tarp he had laid down. He had to admit everything looked fantastic. The firepit was ready to be lit so they'd be cozy.

Taking the porch stairs two at a time, he strode right into the kitchen—but not before he noticed Daphne standing by the front window.

"Hey, Jed. Where are you off to in such a hurry?" The petite redhead had a clipboard in one hand and a tape measure in the other.

"Hi, Daph. Just need to pick something up before I head out again. What are you working on?"

"Plans for Thursday. Annie and I were talking and we want to arrange the tables so it's more family-like. Maybe a big square or something. I'm not sure yet."

"Ah, Thanksgiving with our family of misfits."

She popped a hand on her hip and gave him a saucy smirk. "Family's what you make of it, and I happen to think Annie and Linc along with Mary have done a fine job making our large eclectic brood feel like they belong."

He thought about that statement for a second. "Isn't that the truth. I've seen some people come and they're gone in three months and others stay for years. Look at me. I'm a prime example. Before Pops hired me, I moved around a lot. But stepping foot on this land, I felt like I had come home."

Her face softened. "I get it. I planned on coming out for a visit and the next thing I knew, Annie and I flew to Boston, packed up my things, and here I am—and I've never been happier. Whoever said you can't take the girl out of the city was wrong."

He tipped his hat in a gentlemanly gesture. "I guess that makes us cousins or something."

"I guess it does." She grinned. "Have a good time tonight —and cuz, don't do anything I wouldn't do."

He was sure he blinked hard at the reference to the evening's plans. "Does everyone know?"

"No, but Annie asked me to pick out some wine and craft beer for tonight; something special. Don't worry, your secret is safe."

"Thanks, I guess."

"I like Maggie and she deserves happiness. From what I've heard, she's had it rough, single parent, running the diner, and all. So, like I said, have fun." She pointed to the kitchen. "Quinn's got everything all set."

She didn't need to tell him twice. He had just enough time

to shower and get ready to pick up his date. "See ya later, Daphne."

*J*ed was used to dressing for cold weather, but he wasn't sure about Maggie. He tossed another wool blanket into the back seat of the truck along with the picnic basket Quinn had packed to overflowing. He looked at cabin six. Then he took a deep breath and walked up the stairs and tentatively knocked.

The door opened and Susie stood in the doorway, grinning like a possum eating a sweet potato. "Hi, Jed. Come on in. Mom is almost ready."

He took his hat off and stepped inside. "Thank you." If he wasn't pushing forty, he'd swear he was a teenager again, picking up his first date. He glanced around the room and noticed the feminine touches that had been added over the last several weeks. The ladies had made this their home.

"Where are you and Mom going tonight?"

"A picnic."

"I see, and where might this picnic be taking place?" she asked, crossing her arms over her stomach and grinning even wider.

Maggie bit back a laugh; her shoulders shook slightly with the effort. "Outside." *Two could play at this game.*

"Huh. A little chilly out tonight. How do you plan on staying warm?"

He could see laughter dancing in her brown eyes. "I have my ways." The corners of his mouth begin to twitch upward.

"Have her home by ten. It's a work night and all."

"Susie." Maggie came down the short hall wearing jeans, a turtleneck sweater, and a long fleece jacket. "Stop torturing Jed with your attempt at humor."

He liked that she was coming to his defense, but the little minx wasn't anyone he couldn't handle and he liked bantering with Susie. "It's fine. She was asking about our dinner plans."

Maggie's brow quirked. "Remember who's the parent in this group." She pointed to Susie and back at herself. "But if you need something, I'll have my cell with me. Dinner is in the oven."

"No worries, Mom. I'm going down to the barn and do a few chores, and then I'll have dinner. You guys stay out as late as you want. No need to rush home on my account."

Maggie kissed her on the cheek.

"Have fun." Susie poked Jed in the arm. "Look after my momma."

Jed smiled at Susie and then turned to Maggie. "You can count on it." He opened the door and Maggie grabbed a heavy winter coat from the hook.

"Night," Susie said as Jed closed the door.

*M*aggie zipped her heavy coat. "I'm sorry about all of that. I guess she's giving me a taste of my own words when I ask her questions before she goes out."

"That doesn't bother me." He took her hand as they walked down the steps in the direction of his truck. "I think it's nice she's invested in your happiness."

"And I think it's sweet you're so patient with her."

He opened the truck door. "Now that we've got all the nice and sweet stuff out of the way…" He lowered his lips to hers and kissed her softly. When he stopped, he said, "Hello. You look beautiful tonight."

The dome light inside the truck illuminated her cheeks which flushed a sweet shade of pink.

When she looked him in the eye, his breath caught in his chest. She really was stunning; her blue eyes always did him in.

"Hello, cowboy. I was thinking. If it's too cold out, we can do something else."

He held out his hand and helped her into the passenger seat. "I think you'll be happy when you see our picnic setup. Do you trust me?"

She didn't hesitate. "With my life."

He closed the door and strode around the back. *With luck tonight was hopefully the first of many with Maggie.*

On the drive over to the lean-to, Maggie filled him in on what had happened with Monty Johnson earlier and that he was arranging to send five more carpenters to help speed up the construction.

"Are you sure he's legit?" Jed flicked on his blinker as he turned up the gravel road heading toward the old Grace house.

"After he left, Jesse and I checked him out online and I also talked with Cora at the bank. He's very wealthy and does have four kids. Sounds like he raised them on his own after his wife passed, so I'm guessing he overindulged them. But either way, I appreciate adding people to the crew. That means it will go even faster." She gazed out her window. "Are we at Annie's parents' place?"

"We are. There happens to be a great spot to watch the moon and stars."

"But isn't this where…" Her question died on her lips when he took her hand.

"Don't worry. This place didn't hurt me and Polly. A man did, and he's rotting in jail. I refuse to let what happened change how I live my life." He gave her hand a squeeze. "Well, except no one's ever going to get the jump on me again. I ignored my instincts and let my guard down, but that was the first and last time."

He parked the truck as close as he could get to the picnic spot. Kissing the back of her gloved hand, he said, "Are you ready for our evening to begin?"

A slow, shy smile slid from one side of her mouth to the other. "Yes."

With one simple word, he was a total goner. *This really is the only woman for me. Slow down, cowboy. Give her time to fall for you, too.*

He carried the basket in one hand, holding hers in the other. Her gasp was audible the moment she saw the lean-to with a soft glow from battery-operated candles and someone had come and lit the fire. Smiling to himself, he'd have to thank Linc in the morning. He glanced around, sure Annie and Linc were close since they wouldn't have left the fire unattended. But he didn't see anyone.

"Jed, this is the most romantic thing that anyone has ever done for me." Standing on tiptoe, she brushed his lips with hers. "It's just perfect."

His voice was husky as he said, "You inspire me, but I did have a little help from Annie, Linc, Daphne, and Quinn. I guess it takes help from my family to sweep you off your feet." Dropping the picnic basket, he slid his arms around her waist and deepened the kiss.

23

*M*aggie's eyes widened. The scene for their date was something out of a magazine spread for *Amazing Montana Living*. Or better yet, a picnic fit for a queen. There was a table for two set with a bouquet of greens and red holly berries just inside what couldn't even be called a simple shelter. As she walked closer, she took in every detail from the thick rug on the ground to heavy drapes flanking the entrance, an arrangement of cushions and pillows for reclining with a full view of the sky and the crackling fire. Inside, it was warmer than she thought it would be, wrapping around her like a warm embrace. For a heartbeat, she almost felt she'd been whisked away to a far-off land, pausing on the journey to enjoy a luxurious meal fit for royalty.

"You outdid yourself." She held out her hand for him and drew him closer. "It's magical. Would you mind if I took a couple of pictures? I don't ever want to forget even the smallest detail."

He smiled. "You can do whatever you want; it's your night."

"No." She brought the back of her hand to his cheek and held it there. "It's ours."

Jed said, "I'm going to set up our supper if you want to do your picture thing, and then we can eat whenever you're hungry."

She withdrew her phone and did a slow three-sixty, taking pictures, and she even snuck in a video of Jed arranging their meal. Then Maggie walked outside and took a few more pictures of the shelter before turning to take in the spectacular view. She could feel the warmth emanating from Jed as he came up behind her and she leaned into his chest as his arms slipped around her waist.

"Breathtaking." A few stars had begun to twinkle in the darkening sky and the moon was above the horizon, making its way upward. They stood watching the sky in the crisp fall air as the fire crackled. It was as if they were the only two people in the world.

"Are you hungry? Would you like some wine or even a beer?"

His breath was warm on her cheek and a flicker of nerves skittered in her stomach. "Wine would be nice. Shall we sit by the fire?"

"There's a comfy log bench for that very purpose." He walked her over and said, "I'll be right back."

Maggie wasn't used to being waited on and started to follow him, but he pointed to the bench. "Relax, please."

She did as he asked and returned to the bench but tossed a log onto the fire before settling down. Taking her gloves off, she stuffed them in her coat pockets, and held her hands to the fire. She couldn't even begin to put into words how she was feeling right now. *Don't overanalyze everything just roll with the flow.*

Jed came back and stepped over the bench before sitting close to her, thigh to thigh. He handed her a glass of wine, and she was surprised to discover it wasn't plastic. "Fancy." She sipped and was pleased to taste a light fruity white. Something she would have picked out.

He tapped his beer bottle to her glass. "I hope we have more nights like this."

Maggie looked at him and smiled. "You can count on it." Of the handful of dates she'd had in the last twenty years, Jed was by far the best man she had ever gone out with.

They sat in comfortable silence for a few minutes, but it wasn't awkward. They had known each other casually a long time and Jed was a man of few words, but what he said mattered.

He took a sip of his beer. "Is Susie finding ranch life a little better now that she's fallen in love with horses?"

"I think so. She would prefer to be closer to her friends, but I think expanding her horizons with learning to ride and even the barrel racing is important overall."

Jed studied the dancing flames. "It's good that you're supportive. I know the whole idea of her learning to race scares you—and not from the actual act of racing. That does have its own dangers, but she's not her father and you've done a great job raising her. I'm confident Susie will find the right path for her."

Sipping her wine, she thought about what he had said. "Are you speaking from personal experience?"

"When you're a kid, the only people who should always have your back are your folks and when they don't, that can damage how you look at life."

He got up and poked at the fire, tossing another log on, although it didn't seem to Maggie like it needed one, yet. There was more to the story than he was saying, and *I wanted to ask questions, but that was one sure way to have him shut down. Was it worth the risk?*

"Your parents weren't supportive of your life choices?"

He shook his head. "No. But I don't want this to put a dark cloud over tonight. Maybe we can we talk about it some other time?"

She touched his arm. "Of course." *It's not my place to judge but his family must have hurt him terribly.* "Are you hungry yet?" She stood. "I'm dying to taste what Quinn whipped up for us." Slipping her arm through the crook of his, she said, "Do you think he packed dessert, too?"

Chuckling, he said, "I'm sure. What's a picnic without something sweet?" He pecked her lips. "Besides you."

"You keep saying things like that, cowboy, and you'll never get rid of me."

He tipped his head to one side, giving her a thoughtful look. "Would that be so bad?"

With her heartbeat kicking into a gallop, she pulled him closer. "No. In fact, I'm thinking it's what all that has happened is leading us to. They say out of something bad comes something good."

He lowered his mouth to hers and, before kissing her, he paused. "I would agree that is a true statement."

*D*inner had been amazing. Quinn had packed fried chicken slider sandwiches, homemade pickles, and tangy coleslaw with apple slivers. And for dessert, he sent graham cookies with chunks of chocolate and a bag of marshmallows for an amped-up version of s'mores. She would never have thought to create a cookie base for them, but it had worked perfectly when she and Jed toasted marshmallows and added more dark chocolate.

She leaned against Jed and pulled a heavy wool blanket around them as they sat, while Jed roasted another marshmallow. "I'm not sure I can eat another bite of anything." She sat up straighter as if it would make more room in her belly.

He laughed. "I'm making this for me. You still haven't finished the last one."

She glanced at the small plate next to her and he was right, but the fact he could see it from where he sat only indicated he was very observant.

Tipping her head back, she drank in the night sky. "Will you look at those stars and that moon. I never get tired of it. Maybe I should talk to Tasha about adding a deck on the roof so I could go out and watch the moon come up every night."

"There is something special about moonlight over Montana." He tossed the stick he'd been using for roasting dessert into the fire.

"Where else have you lived besides here?"

He stiffened and before she could find a polite way to say never mind, Jed began to talk. "I grew up in Colorado. Left home after I graduated college. The business degree I had just didn't fit what I wanted to do with my life. So, I worked on a ranch in Texas for a while, then Arizona, found my way to Wyoming, and then eventually parked my truck here."

In that statement, he had said more than he realized. "Your family wanted you to be a businessman?"

"Yeah. When I said I wanted to work the land and with horses, we agreed to part ways. So, now you know I was a family of one until I landed the job with Pops."

Maggie loved how everyone who had met Annie's grandfather referred to him affectionately as Pops. He had been a very special man and had a way of making everyone feel as if they mattered. She put her head on his shoulder. "I'm sorry you had to make a choice like that."

"It is what it is."

"Have you reached out to them at all since being here?"

He cleared his throat. "I send a card every Christmas and for their birthdays—not that I get anything in return, but at least I know I've tried to maintain contact."

Her heart ached for him. "That's all you can do."

He put his arm around her waist and held her tight. "I've never told anyone that, so please keep my secret."

Sitting up straight, she slid her hand beneath his chin, guiding his gaze back to her. "You never have to worry about me oversharing personal information with anyone. That's not my style, and I appreciate that you trusted me enough to tell me."

He lowered his chin, resting his head on her shoulder. Unguarded. Vulnerable. For once, he wasn't the tough cowboy but just a man opening his heart. "It feels good to talk to you like this."

"I promise you, I will let Susie make her own way in the world, even if I don't always agree. The most important thing for me is that she's happy and knows my love for her is unconditional."

When he hugged her, Maggie felt as if the world was finally tilting the way it was always meant to be.

"Unconventional first date conversation."

She laughed softly. "Oh, do you think we missed some important topics? Then, let's get them cleared up. I'm a Gemini; my favorite color is lapis blue; I love daisies and fudge without nuts, but ice cream sundaes must have them. Morning is my favorite time of day with a good cup of coffee and a sunrise. I love books and always read the last chapter first, just to make sure the ending is worthwhile. And I'm partial to a cowboy with gray eyes and a sexy swagger." With a saucy wink, she said, "Your turn."

He pushed his cowboy hat back at bit. "In addition to my favorite foods which, you already know, I'm a Capricorn; I'm colorblind so color doesn't matter much to me. I'm equal opportunity on flowers. Nuts with everything. Anytime of the day is good for me, good coffee is a must, and for me, moonlight has taken on a new fondness. Oh, and I'm partial to a woman with curves who is kind and knows what she wants and isn't afraid to ask for it."

She thought of the moment she'd asked to be kissed. But she wasn't embarrassed. It had gotten them here, hadn't it?

"We have a lot more in common than either of us probably knew." The fire popped and a few sparks danced toward the heavens. "You know I, too, have come to appreciate not just the evening but a crisp night by the fire."

"Are you cold?"

She tipped her head and gave him a side-look. "We could go back and watch the fire from inside our little haven."

He helped her up and they walked in sync. Jed stopped before they reached the entrance. "I'm not looking to rush anything, Maggie. Whatever happens is up to you."

His words made her breath hitch. She wasn't ready to go horizontal with him just yet. The temptation was there as they sat next to the fire; the heat in his kiss ignited a deeper longing. But she wanted to take this budding relationship slow and steady, savoring each moment of discovering each other. They both carried scars and regrets from the past; they deserved something real and lasting.

"If you're not careful, I could really fall for you, cowboy."

He brushed back her hair and gave her a featherweight kiss over her eyes, then along her temples, before finally finding her mouth. His words a light promise against her lips. "Don't worry, I'll catch you when you do."

She sighed. *Who am I trying to kid, I've already fallen. Now to make sure I didn't get hurt.*

24

*L*oud voices from inside the barn caused Jed to break out into a run. Who the heck was carrying on like that around the horses? He rounded the corner and saw the door standing open. Just inside were Maggie and Susie. Last night Susie had been teasing them about their first date and now she was screaming as if all was lost in the world.

"Ladies!" His sharp tone caused them both to focus on him. "What is going on? I can hear you from a mile away." It was an exaggeration, but it was the first thing that popped into his mind. It was something his mom would have said to his sister and him when they were arguing.

Susie threw her hands up in the air. "She won't let me stay in town this weekend and next. I just want to hang out with my friends. And before I get my horse, I want to do stuff."

He could swear he saw a pout forming and right now, Susie looked ten years old, not sixteen. *This was not a fight I wanted to step into the middle of, but I'm getting sucked in like quicksand.*

Maggie shook her head. "I asked her to help me with my orders and when I went into town to check on the diner, I said

I'd drop her off at Mandy's, but she's insisting she has to go now or the world will come to an end." She threw up her hands and walked deeper into the barn.

"Jed, can't you talk to Mom or…" A gleam came into her eyes. "Would you take me into town? The gang is meeting up at the Pizza Ranch for an early lunch, and then we're going to the movies for a double feature. Marcy can bring me back out after dinner." She looked at her mom who had walked back in their direction and said, "Please, Jed. I'll help Mom tomorrow."

He nodded in Maggie's direction. "It's not up to me and I don't want to get caught between a mother and a daughter."

"But you don't think it's an unreasonable ask, do you?"

Locking eyes with Maggie, he cocked a brow. As if asking if it was okay.

"Fine but tomorrow we have to work. I start making deliveries on Monday and this weekend is my big push."

Susie threw her arms around Maggie and squealed. "Thanks, Mom. And I promise I'll get up early and be ready to bake when you give the word."

Maggie looked over her shoulder at Jed. "I'll drive her in; you don't need to."

"It's fine. I was heading in, anyway. I need to swing by The Trading Post."

Susie said, "I want to check on Nahla before we go. Do I have time?"

He liked that she thought about the horse first. "I'll meet you at my truck when you're ready."

Maggie fell into step next to him and they walked out of the barn and Jed slid the heavy door closed. "You don't need to drive her in— especially if you just said you had to go to help me out. I can be her chauffeur."

"I have to go. There's no sense you making the trip, too. And besides, if you get to work, maybe you can finish up early and we can run into The Lucky Bucket for dinner?"

"Are you asking me on a second date?"

He winked. "Are you saying yes?"

"Absolutely. And I'll let Susie know we can pick her up at Marcy's after we're done with dinner if that's okay with you." She placed a hand on his arm. "Not very romantic but practical."

"I'll get my romance fix in before and during dinner." He brushed his lips over hers and he liked how he could kiss her just about whenever he wanted.

"That sounds very promising and The Lucky Bucket will be fun. Maybe we can shoot a game or two of pool."

Susie ran past them to the cabin. "I'll be right back and the sooner we leave, the more fun I can have. Meet you at the truck."

Jed laughed. "She's in a hurry to get to town for pizza and it's not even ten o'clock."

"Teenagers can eat twenty-four hours a day—or have you forgotten what it was like to be sixteen?"

"I remember a few things." He twirled her into his arms, and she placed a hand against his chest.

Her dark-blond eyelashes fluttered as she looked up and said, "I think that's a conversation for another day."

Reluctantly, he released her, but it was one they'd revisit. Susie getting into the passenger seat of the truck caught his eye. "Someone's anxious. I'd better get going."

Maggie gave him a lingering kiss. "Thanks again for helping me out. You made her day, that's for sure."

"I'll see you when I get back." He gave her one last kiss and pulled open the truck door.

Maggie leaned in. "We're going to have dinner at The Lucky Bucket tonight so you can come home with us. Just text me later and let me know whose house you're at."

Her face blanched for a fraction of a second, and Jed wondered what that was all about, before she agreed to text later.

He started the truck and backed up before heading down the gravel driveway. He noticed Susie had a large duffel bag at her feet. "Moving back to town?"

"What?"

He pointed to the bag. "I thought it was just for the day."

"Oh, yeah. Marcy's got a date tomorrow and I said she could borrow something of mine." She put her ear phones on and tapped her cell phone effectively ending that part of the conversation.

Jed remembered his sister and her friends always trading clothes. He thought it was silly but harmless.

When they reached the blacktop, Susie pulled out her earphones. "Jed, have you heard from your friend yet on my horse? I've been talking to Tate, and he's been telling me how we're going to train and I'm excited to get started."

"Not yet. But as soon as he has a lead on a good mount, he'll call." With one hand on the wheel and the other propped on the door, he studied the road. "Are you looking forward to getting back to town once the diner is reopened?"

"Yeah, but the only downside is my horse will be at the ranch so I'll be coming out twice a day to take care of it. But I can get my driver's license in March so at least Mom won't need to drive me around anymore."

"Are you sure you want to have the responsibility of a horse? You'll be going off to college in a couple of years."

"Maybe not. If I get really good, I can make money working the rodeo. I've been asking around and I'll bet I could make enough to support me and my horse."

He was hearing the words but what more was behind them? "Does your mom know this is a possibility?"

Susie looked out the windshield, doing her best not to look right or left. "She wants me to go to college and until I make some decisions, I've decided to not bring the topic up." She snapped her head in his direction. "You're not going to tell her, are you?"

"What's to tell? You're undecided about your future other than you still want to learn barrel racing and have your own horse. But you should still keep your grades up in school and have some fun, too."

She exhaled. "That's why I really wanted to go into town today and experience all I can. Meet people, talk about life, you know all that interesting stuff."

There was much more to her thought process than met the eye, but he wasn't about to scare Maggie half to death with a gut feeling that something was off. What he *would* do is keep an open eye and ear and if anything were going wonky with Susie, he'd be there to step in. Sure, she was Maggie's daughter, but Jed also looked at her as extended family in the short time they'd been living at the ranch. He could see she had a big heart just like her mom and she was smart and a hard worker. All those qualities deserved trust and loyalty. He just prayed she wouldn't run off half-cocked and do something she'd regret down the road.

"Is there a male friend that you're meeting today?"

A flicker of panic crossed her face. "What makes you ask that?"

"You're sixteen and, believe it or not, I was sixteen once, too. Itching to hang out with friends for me usually meant someone special would be there, too."

Jed glanced at her as relief flickered in her eyes. "Yeah, there is. But don't tell Mom. I'm not ready to spring the news on her, yet."

Dang, now he had to ask a few more questions just to make sure nothing was going to turn bottom side up. "He's not putting any pressure on you of any kind, is he?"

"No. No, Jed, he's not like that. He's a really nice guy and we're just talking, you know, getting to know each other. We've been talking online a little bit and today we're going to hang out."

"Right, pizza and a movie. Sounds more like a date to

me." He gave her an encouraging smile, hoping she'd tell him a little more, like the kid's name.

"It's not like that. I'm not looking for a serious boyfriend, so stop worrying. I told you it's all good stuff."

During this conversation, he wondered if this was how his father felt when his sister had been sixteen and started to date. If only he could call him—but that wasn't an option. Jed was on his own to navigate being the boyfriend of this girl's mother.

"Did you and Mom have a good time last night?"

"We did. Quinn made us dinner and we ate by a fire while watching the stars and moon."

She gave a low whistle. "Pulling out all the stops, Jed. Nicely done. I'll bet Mom swooned just a little bit."

"It was nice." He was not going to reveal the details of the date...not to Susie or anyone. If Maggie wanted to tell her, then she could.

"Be patient with her. She and my dad didn't have the best relationship. He left when I was just a newborn, and I don't know that Mom ever got over his leaving. They were just two different people who wanted different lives."

He wasn't sure who Susie was protecting, her mother or the deadbeat father. Maybe she had romanticized their relationship into something like a Greek tragedy when it wasn't. As far as he was concerned, any man who walked out on his child was not a man.

"I can promise you I will always treat Maggie with respect. The best part of our relationship is we've been friends for a long time."

"I read in a magazine that the best love affairs are also best friends."

He almost choked when she used the word affair. That word was best ignored. "I agree the best relationships do have a strong friend component."

She made a *hmm* sound and looked out the window.

Turning back and giving him a pointed look, she asked, "Do you plan on sticking around?"

"Are you asking me what my intentions are toward your mother?"

"I guess I am, and they are?"

"I like Maggie and as long as she and I are enjoying each other's company, I plan on seeing her. Does that answer your question?"

Her brows knitted together. "Even after I'm gone?"

"I have no idea where we'll be in two years, but I can't see why we wouldn't still be close." Jed wasn't sure if that was the way she wanted him to answer. Even if he could see a long-term future with Maggie, he didn't know if she could. At least not yet.

Susie smiled and seemed satisfied with his answer.

He slowed as they turned onto Main Street.

"Can you drop me in front of the pharmacy?" She looked around the area. "And what time do you think you and Mom will be going home tonight?"

"Around eight maybe? Does that give you enough time to have fun?"

"It does." She had her hand on the door and then slid across the bench seat and gave him a one-armed hug. "Thanks, Jed." She got out of the truck, dragging the duffel bag with her, and slammed the door. He saw her in the rearview mirror standing on the sidewalk watching him drive away.

25

*I*t was Thanksgiving morning and when Maggie woke, the air chilly as she inhaled and stretched. She tugged a blanket around her shoulders and shuffled into the hall. The thermostat was stuck on fifty degrees, she tapped it and nudged it to seventy. Shaking her head at how it got so low. In the living room she knelt next to the wood stove, stacked paper, kindling and small logs and lit it. Rubbing her hands together in front of the tiny flames. *Hopefully the place will warm up quick. Until then, coffee for me and a mug of cocoa for Susie will take the chill off.*

As she measured grounds into the pot a smile tugged at the corners of her mouth. The busy week of working as a team baking and delivering orders had drawn them closer, more like before the fire. She tiptoed down the hall and softly tapped on Susie's bedroom door.

She said, "Happy Thanksgiving," as she eased open the door. Susie was sprawled under the covers. Her long blond hair was in a braid. She had said she wanted it to have some waves today and this was the easiest way to make it happen.

"Suz."

She waved a hand at Maggie. "Go away."

"Cocoa will be ready soon."

She opened one eye and looked at Maggie. "Not the dry packet stuff? With real whipped cream?"

"My special holiday recipe with lots of cream." She turned and was going to close the door but looked over her shoulder. "You're not going to let it get cold now, are you?"

Susie sat up in bed and rubbed a hand over her eyes. The action reminded Maggie of when she was tiny and did that very same thing. Her heart twisted with nostalgia. *Oh, the good times.*

"I'll be out soon."

Maggie closed the door and waited until she heard feet hit the floor. Now she'd whip up something creamy and chocolaty. After all, it was a holiday tradition.

*S*usie was watching the parade on television when she called out, "Hey, Mom. Come look at this."

Maggie came in carrying a tray with two mugs of cocoa and a plate with muffins and sliced fruit. She pulled the blanket across her lap as she sat down. "What are we watching?"

"I know you like seeing the Rockettes and they're coming up next." She took a mug and stuck her finger into the whipped cream and licked it off. "Yum."

They watched the parade, the floats and bands rolled across the screen but the air was heavy with the aroma of coffee, cocoa and wood smoke. It was the first year in many the homey smells of roasting turkey and sage dressing didn't waft from the kitchen. She sighed, *Next year.*

Susie was nibbling on a slice of apple. "What time do we need to walk over to the dining room?"

"We should go up around eleven. I offered to help Quinn get the turkeys in the oven but he was being protective of the birds—so, I figure later this morning, we can help with sides, set the tables, and arrange the centerpieces. Also, I think Annie and Daphne will be down around the same time."

"That'll be fun. What's the story with Daphne? Is she going to live at the big house forever?"

Maggie glanced at Susie. "I don't know and it's none of my business. What I do know is you need to get in the shower so we'll be ready to go on time."

She got off the couch. "Fine, but I'm not peeling potatoes." Grinning, she picked up her mug of cocoa. "This hit the spot. Thanks, Mom."

"Save me some hot water." Maggie sighed. The day was starting off at a slow, easy pace. Every time she began to relax, the thought of *what's the next bomb*, fear crept in. The diner's ashes left coated her soul. Even with all the good things that followed, her life felt out of balance, and one wrong move would knock her down again.

Susie's cell vibrated on the coffee table and Maggie picked it up. She didn't recognize the number. Her finger hesitated over the answer button but instead, she changed her mind and put it back down. *It must be a wrong number.* She waited to see if the phone pinged with an incoming message, but it didn't. Satisfied it was a mistake, she picked up the tray and went to tidy the efficiency kitchen. *One thing I wouldn't miss when we moved back to town was the apartment-size stove and refrigerator. But the downside was, Jed wouldn't be next door.*

*M*aggie and Susie came out of their cabin and Jed came out of his at the same time.

Susie looked from one to the other. "Did you guys plan this?"

Maggie slung her arm over Susie's shoulders. "Of course we did."

Jed jogged down the steps and took Maggie's hand as they walked in the direction of the dining hall.

Susie fell in step next to Jed. "You know, I've been wondering about something."

Jed looked at her. "And what might that be?"

"How come no one here ever drives to a meal? We see people just walking like zombies following the smell of food."

He chuckled. "You've eaten Quinn's food. It sticks to your ribs and the ranch hands don't want to have to buy new clothes every six months, so they indulge and then walk some of the extra calories off."

"Good point." She pointed to a truck kicking up dust on the road in. "Hey, that looks like Clint and Polly."

Maggie turned her head. "How do you know everyone's vehicles?"

"I spend time at the barn, remember, and people are always coming and going. Mom, you need to get out of the kitchen more and experience all that ranch life has to offer."

She clutched her chest in mock surprise. "Who are you and what have you done with my daughter?"

"It's no biggie. I realized I'm pretty lucky to be able to stay on this ranch, learn to ride, and meet so many nice people." She beamed at Jed. "Especially you."

He tapped the rim of his cowboy hat. "Thank you kindly." He added a deep drawl which made Susie laugh.

The trio climbed the wide steps to the dining hall and despite the cold, there were several windows cracked and the smells coming from inside caused Maggie's mouth to water. "Is it always like this for a holiday meal?"

"Christmas is even better. Just wait and see for yourself."

I liked how that sounded.

He held the door for her and Susie.

Once they were inside and got their coats hung on a couple of free hooks, Susie made a beeline for Mary who was sitting on a leather sofa overlooking the entire ranch. As Maggie watched, she had a twist of sadness that her parents were in Arizona for the holiday, but the cold bothered her dad's arthritis and they were nervous about snowstorms and driving. Dad never developed a fondness for air travel. It seemed that Mary was a surrogate grandmother today and by the look on hers and Susie's faces, it was a perfect match. Mary kissed Susie's cheek as they put their heads together, and laughter drifted across the room.

"Hey, pretty lady, are you ready to dive into kitchen duty?" Jed bent low to her ear. "And you are very pretty today in this burgundy sweater."

She let her gaze take in all of Jed's cowboy-ness from his boots to his just tight enough Wranglers and heavy flannel shirt. "You're not so bad yourself."

Annie interrupted their mutual assessment with a quick hug for each of them. "Come on into the kitchen. Quinn is waiting on both of you."

Jed's gray eyes twinkled. "Ma'am, we'll follow you."

Annie winked at Maggie. "Darn tootin' he will."

As Jed had mentioned, Daphne rearranged the tables in one large square in the middle of the room. Someone had started a fire in the large fieldstone fireplace that dominated one wall. As everyone gathered around the table, people were in high spirits, laughing and joking. Maggie wasn't surprised to see that Jed had been right; it was like a large family. Complete with the kindly uncle types who would protect everyone in this room and jokesters dropping rapid-fire jokes, causing Susie, to laugh so hard she held her belly as tears rolled down her cheeks. She had grown comfortable at the ranch, and it wasn't just for show from what she had said earlier today.

Annie and Linc took their seats in the middle of one side. Mary sat to the right of Annie and Daphne was on Linc's left. It was easy to see they were the nucleus to all that surrounded them. Without Annie's strong but gentle hand in running the ranch, it would have folded after her grandfather passed and with Linc by her side, they made an unbeatable team.

She clinked her water glass with her knife as she stood. The din in the room quieted and all eyes were riveted to her.

Jed had taken Maggie's hand under the table, and Susie grinned at them from the other side.

"Thank you, everyone, for coming to another Grace Star Ranch holiday meal prepared in large part by the incomparable Quinn with a little help from everyone else in the room."

A smattering of laughter filled the air.

"And Daphne for changing things up with how we share this time together. I think this setup will become a new part of our tradition here." Her gaze slid from one person to the next. "It's been a busy year. We've had some adventures with construction on the new dude ranch section. And if you missed the rumor mill, we're on track to open in May. There is one thing I want to assure you. All major holidays—Thanksgiving, Christmas, New Year's, and Easter—will always be reserved for our family, which each person sitting at this table is a treasured member of."

A couple of hoots rang out in response to her last statement.

"In addition, we've had our share of joy. Our palomino horse family is expanding thanks to Jed, Tate, and Zak. Vegetables on our table are courtesy of our very own Polly. And today, we welcome two more people into our family fold, Maggie and Susie Brady, who found their way to the ranch due to a horrible fire but they're here—safe and sound—and it's because of Maggie that we've all had to add some extra walking into our days with her baked goods."

A few of the guys started to chant, "Maggie. Maggie."

Annie held up her hand. "Just thank her later for I have

one more announcement regarding family." She looked at Linc and he took her hand.

Maggie could feel her smile grow. She knew what Annie and Linc wanted to share.

"In March we will be welcoming the next generation to our family. Linc and I are going to have a baby." Tears filled her eyes as Mary rose to her feet and wrapped her arms around her. She was saying something, and Annie was nodding.

"Mary just asked if I was serious that she was finally going to be a Gigi, and of course that is a heck yeah." Linc walked around Annie and gathered the old woman in his arms as she wept tears of joy. "So on this day, we all have so much to be thankful for. But I want you to know, from the bottom of my heart—and I speak for Linc, Mary, and Daphne—we would not be the family we are without each and every one of you." She placed her hand over her heart and her voice was thick with emotion as she said, "Thank you."

The moment she sat down, everyone began to talk, and food was temporarily forgotten in the excitement of the announcement.

Maggie was amazed. If she hadn't seen the reaction of all who were gathered around this table, she wouldn't have believed it. Looking at Susie, she too had tears in her eyes. She mouthed, *I love you, Momma. Always and forever.*

26

Stuffed from his toes to the brim of his hat, Jed walked home with Maggie and Susie to cabin number six. He studied the sky before they went inside. "There's a bad storm brewing."

Maggie gave him a worried look. "Tonight?"

"No, I'm guessing it will hit us later tomorrow night. If you need any supplies, we'd best go into town first thing in the morning and get what you need. Blizzards are bad in town, but out here, we can get cut off for a couple of days. So, we need to make sure we're self-sufficient." He glanced at Susie. "Maybe in the morning you can help me bring in extra wood and we'll stack more on the porch."

She glanced at Maggie. "I was going to that sleepover this weekend. Can I still go?"

"Honey, if Jed's right, I'd like to have you with me, where I know you're safe."

She pushed open the door with a bang. "I can't believe you're going to let a little snow be a buzzkill." Not waiting for them to come in, she slammed the door.

Maggie's face went from blank to anger in a heartbeat. "Jed, I'm sorry, but I need to get inside and talk to my daughter. It seems not only has she forgotten her manners, but also her common sense when it comes to winter weather."

Taking her by the shoulders, he pulled her in for a tender kiss good night. "Call if you need anything. I'm going to check on the horses one last time, but I'm around."

"Thanks for understanding. I really had a great time today. Thanks for asking me to come."

"You and Susie belong here, Mags. You heard Annie, you two are family."

She went up the steps and gave him a small, sad wave before going inside. He lingered at the bottom of the stairs, wondering if Susie would storm out and take off to parts unknown on the ranch like she did when they first moved out there. Instead of heading toward the barn, Jed crossed the short space between the cabins and sat on his porch. He had time to wait and see what might happen next.

*L*ater that night, his cell phone pinged. He glanced at the screen and smiled.

Meet me on your porch…

He didn't have to be asked twice. He pulled on a hooded sweatshirt, jeans, and his boots and—without turning on the lights—went out the door. Sitting on the bench was Maggie. She held up a mug and he could see wisps of steam rising in the glow of the moon. Sitting next to her, he took the mug, kissed her cheek, and wrapped his arm around her all in one fell swoop. "This is a nice surprise."

"After talking with Susie, I was too keyed up to sleep, so naturally I thought to text you."

"Because you think I never sleep?" He sipped the chocolaty beverage; it was delicious and he could taste a shot of peppermint schnapps lingering in the background. *This is my kind of cocoa.*

"No, because when I looked out the window, I saw a light on and you moving around. I figured if you were still up, we could spend some time together."

"I like how you think." He tapped his mug to hers. "Want to talk about the fight with your daughter?"

"You know, we've argued before when I put guidelines in place. She calls them inflexible rules, but I'm the parent and all I want is for her to be safe. If she's staying at a friend's house during a storm, how will I know for sure she's okay?" She looked at Jed. "Ever since the fire, I've had this irrational fear that I am going to lose her and it's turned me into a helicopter mom, which I've never wanted to be. I know it's upsetting to her, but we both could have died if it wasn't for you being in town."

She shuddered and he tightened his arm around her shoulders. "But I was there, and you and Susie are safe. I've been thinking—and if you feel I'm overstepping just say so."

"No. I'd like to hear what you have to say."

"We should go into town tomorrow and pick up a few things. What if we took Susie with us? She could hang out with her friends for a while and when we're ready to come back to the ranch, we'll swing by Marcy's and pick her up. She'll have something that she wants, and you can have her with you here."

Maggie sipped her cocoa and Jed didn't push her for a response. They had until the sun came up if necessary.

"Compromise is the key to success in all relationships, even between mothers and daughters." She kissed his cheek, causing him to smile.

"Does this mean I had a good idea?"

"I just wish I had thought of it. We were each too busy arguing our points that a compromise was never considered. I'll talk to her about it when she gets up."

"Good. I'll check in with Linc to make sure and get whatever they need, too. No sense in all of us heading to town." He drank the last of his cocoa and set the mug aside. "That was really tasty, especially the zip of peppermint."

"I'm glad you enjoyed it." She snuggled closer to his side. "Want to come for breakfast and propose your compromise to Susie? She might be more receptive to the idea if you present it since I'm pretty sure she'll still be upset with me."

"I can do that. You know, I was thinking the last weekend when she was with Marcy she had a duffel bag, but she didn't bring it home with her. Maybe she forgot it."

Maggie pulled away from the crook of his arm and sat up. "What was in it?"

"She said Marcy had a date and wanted to borrow something to wear. My sister and her friends used to do the same thing, but I remember my mother getting annoyed since the clothes rarely found their way back into her closet."

"Good point. Since I wasn't privy to that, feel free to bring it up." Maggie covered her mouth and yawned. "I'm exhausted. It's time to say good night."

Jed pulled her up and held her against him. Kissing her softly, he murmured, "I'll walk you home."

She laughed softly. "It's like forty feet to my steps."

"It's dark and besides, I'd like to savor this moment with you. Once the diner is finished, you will be moving home and we won't have nights like this."

Placing a hand on his chest, she kissed him again. He loved Maggie with all his heart, and he'd savor every moment they were together. *Life is fleeting and can change in an instant.* He'd seen it working the ranch. People got hurt, or worse, and he didn't want to live his life with any more regrets.

"Don't worry, Jed. It won't be like this but other moments just as wonderful will. Now that we've discovered each other, I don't plan on losing you."

He held her tight in his arms, his emotions rolling over him like the river in spring rushing with melting snow runoff. "I'm glad we're on the same page." He kissed the top of her head. "Come on. I'll walk you home."

Jed tucked his list of needed supplies in his shirt pocket. Linc had added a few things and he'd need a couple of stops to get it all done, but at the most, they'd be in town a few hours. Maybe he could convince Maggie to grab pizza for an early lunch before picking up Susie. Taking a look around, he double-checked the woodstove to make sure it would be safe while he was gone and then grabbed his heavy coat, gloves, and hat before going next door.

Susie pulled the door open just as his boots clomped on the top step. "Jed, you're just in time for breakfast. Mom whipped up huckleberry pancakes and sausage."

His stomach growled with anticipation, and he couldn't help but smile. That was one of his favorite breakfasts and Maggie knew it. "Morning, Susie. You look like you're ready to take on the day."

"Every day is a new adventure, you know." She shut the door and gave it an extra push to make sure it was secured. "Did you see the sunrise this morning? It was so fiery-looking —beautiful but intense at the same time."

"That's the storm. My mom always said, 'red sky in morning, take warning.'"

Maggie came out of the tiny kitchen holding three mugs— one had tea and the other two, coffee. "Morning."

Jed leaned in to give her a chaste kiss. Enough to connect but not too much to cause an issue for Susie. Best to let her get used to their relationship slowly. "Thanks, and I hear pancakes are on the griddle."

"Breakfast will be ready in a few minutes."

He noticed the small table was set for three and he wasn't sure if he should broach the idea of Susie's abbreviated visit with her friends now or wait.

"Jed." Susie sat down on a chair and pointed to the couch. "Can I ask your opinion on something?"

He glanced at Maggie who lifted one shoulder and shrugged. He was betting she didn't know what was on Susie's mind either.

"Sure, what's up?"

"I wanted to apologize for last night. I sounded like a real brat when Mom and I were arguing, and you didn't need to see me in action. I don't want you to think that I'm someone who throws a tantrum every time I don't get my way."

He could feel Maggie watching him. Now was a good time to broach the idea of a compromise. "I understand that you were upset with your mom when said she wanted you to be here during the storm."

Susie opened her mouth, and Jed gave her a stern look. He wanted to finish before they discussed it.

"I also understand you like spending time with your friends, so how about a compromise? I'm going into town to get supplies for the ranch, and I've asked your mom to come with me. I thought, if you wanted, we can drop you off at Marcy's and you can hang out for a few hours. When we're done, we can pick you up and bring you back to the ranch before the storm hits. This way, you and your mom both get what you need from the day."

"Really? I can go into town with you?" Susie looked from Jed to Maggie.

She set a plate of pancakes on the table. "Go text Marcy, and then we'll have breakfast. If it's okay with her mom, we can drop you off in about an hour."

She jumped to her feet and threw her arms around Jed's neck. "You're the best, thanks." Withdrawing her cell from her jeans pocket, she jotted off a message. "I'm starving. We should eat. And don't worry, Mom, I'll clean up."

Jed smiled at Maggie. His first attempt at compromise with a teenage girl had worked out well. "And after we get through the storm, I'll check in with Ford Shepard and see how he's making out finding you a horse."

Susie beamed. "This is the best day ever."

He chuckled and said, "Pancakes, a trip to town, and a blizzard. It's definitely going to be eventful."

aggie and Jed had finished gathering all needed supplies and were eating lunch when he noticed it was beginning to snow. "We should get Susie from the library and head back to the ranch before the roads get bad."

They paid the check and now she peered out of the truck windshield after she sent a text to Susie to be ready and waiting on the steps. Five minutes later, Jed pulled up in front of the large brick building and the steps were empty. "I'll just run in and get her."

Dashing up the wide stone steps, she pulled on the door, but it was locked. She cupped her hand around her eyes and peered inside, but there were only security lights illuminated, and then she noticed a paper on the glass with a handwritten note.

Closing early due to storm.

Withdrawing her phone, she hit the speed dial button for Susie. It went straight to voicemail. She tamped down the annoyance tinged with a finger of worry as she hurried back to the truck.

Jed asked, "What's happening?"

"The library closed early, and I tried to call Susie, but it went straight to voicemail. Can we drive by Marcy's? Her parents' house is on the same street where Polly and Clint live."

He dropped the truck in gear and eased away from the curb. There was a thin blanket of snow covering the lawns as they drove and the edges of the blacktop were white with a thin blanket of snow.

Maggie said, "It's the next house on the right."

He put on his blinker and coasted into the ice slicked driveway. Her seat belt was off, and she had the door open before he had fully stopped. The walkway had a half inch of snow and it had only been less than twenty minutes since it started. Jed had been right; this was going to get bad fast.

She depressed the doorbell and then knocked. Doing her best to stay calm, she forced a smile when the door opened. Jessica, Marcy's mom, smiled when she saw her.

"This is a surprise, Maggie. Come in out of the cold."

"I can't stay. I came to pick up Susie."

A puzzled expression settled on Jessica's face. "Susie isn't here. We haven't seen her in quite some time."

A sinking feeling hit her stomach. "You saw her last weekend."

Shaking her head, she called over her shoulder for Marcy. "No. Susie wasn't here over the weekend."

Marcy appeared from another room and when she saw Maggie, her face paled. "Hi, Ms. Brady."

"Have you seen Susie today?"

"No, ma'am. I asked her to come over, but she said she had plans."

A shiver of fear raced down Maggie's spine. "And last weekend?"

"No. A bunch of us got together and we went to the movies, but Susie said she wasn't able to come with us. Something about riding lessons."

"How long has it been since you hung out with her?" Maggie could hear the panic in her voice, but she didn't care.

Jed touched her arm. "Maggie, what's going on?"

Blinking tears from her eyes, she stumbled back a step. "Susie isn't here. She never was."

He looked from Maggie to Marcy. "You didn't meet her at the library this morning?" Before she could answer, he said, "Did you ask to borrow some clothes for a date last Saturday?"

The girl's voice wavered. "No, sir. I haven't seen Susie outside of school in weeks. It was right after the fire that she stopped hanging out with us. We figured it was because she was living on the ranch and it was hard with everything that happened."

Jessica put her arm around her daughter. "Maggie, I'm really sorry. We can start calling all of the girls' friends and see if anyone knows anything."

Maggie nodded, not trusting herself to speak. Jed thanked them and asked if they learned anything to call him and he gave them his cell number.

Marcy said, "Ms. Brady, I'll get the word out."

She nodded and Jed wrapped his arm around her waist and half carried her to the truck. Once he got her inside and buckled up, he got in. "We're going to the sheriff's office."

Tears flowed down her cheeks. "Jed, where is she? It's not safe to be out in this storm."

He took her hand. "I don't know, but we will find her. I promise you that." He pulled out his cell. "I'm calling Linc. I'll have everyone start searching all the buildings at the ranch in case she made her way back there."

She didn't trust herself to speak as Jed drove through the blanket of snow. Shivering, she jammed her hands into her coat pockets. *Where is my little girl?* The words rolled over and over in her head as she stared out the side window.

When they arrived at the sheriff's office, Jed parked as close as he could to the front door. He looked at her, clasping her hand. "Ready?"

"Yes." She pulled a hat onto her head, trying to remember what Susie had on for a coat. Did she take her hat and gloves? What about boots? The temperature was dropping fast and the wind was kicking up.

Jed opened the door to the police station and she walked in, stamping her feet to get the snow off her boots before walking across the floor. Tye Blackstone came out of his office and did a double take.

"Maggie, if this is about the fire, I don't have any information yet."

"Susie's missing." She watched his face freeze in place.

He stepped back and gestured toward his office. "Come inside and tell me exactly what happened."

Jed took her elbow and guided her to a chair. He sat next to her, for which she was grateful, and he reached for her hand.

"We dropped her at the library around ten. She said she was going to hang out with Marcy while we did some errands and we were to pick her up when we were done. I sent her a text and called her, both of which went unanswered. When we got to the library, it was closed due to the storm so we drove over to Marcy's house, figuring the girls were there." She struggled to keep from crying. "But Marcy hasn't seen Susie since school got out and even last weekend when Susie had said she was hanging out with their group, Marcy said she didn't come." She squeezed Jed's hand. "But that's what she told us."

Jed said, "Also, there's the duffel bag that she took with her last weekend."

The sheriff perched on the edge of his desk. "Tell me more."

"I drove her to town on Saturday and she had a large duffel bag with her. When I asked her, she said Marcy wanted to borrow some clothes for a date. I didn't think much about it given that teenage girls swap clothes, but since we know she was lying about being with her friends, it makes me wonder what was in the bag."

The sheriff nodded. "Typically, we have to wait twenty-four hours before we file a missing person report, but given that Susie is a minor and we have a blizzard hitting us, I'm going to do it now."

Maggie's insides relaxed just a bit. People were going to start looking for her daughter. "Marcy is calling all of their friends to see if anyone has heard from her."

Tye gave a brisk nod. "Good." He turned to Jed. "I'm assuming you've already called the ranch?"

"Yes, they've started to look for her. Once I hear back from Linc, I will let you know."

"What else can we do?" Maggie didn't have to look at Jed; he would be right by her side until Susie was home safe.

He clenched his fist. "Don't tell us to go back to the ranch and wait. That's not going to happen."

He clasped his hands on the top of his leg. "I figured. My people are going to be stretched thin with the storm and under normal circumstances I wouldn't advise you to do anything but wait. However, in this case, can you start with the stores near the library and ask if anyone has seen her or a stranger around? If someone tells you they have seen anything, let me know right away. In the case of a vehicle, probe for the best description possible."

Maggie stood up with Jed mirroring her. "We'll start right now. And please, if you hear anything at all, call me or Jed. You have our numbers from the fire, right?"

"I do." He rested a hand on his belt.

She felt all color drain from her face. "Do you think this is connected to the fire? Could the person who burned down the diner have taken Susie?"

"That's highly unlikely. They are very different scenarios."

"You mean crimes, right?" Maggie's heart felt as if the vise that had started to compress it was getting tighter by the second.

"We're not going to jump to any conclusions. Susie may have gone off with a boy for the day, not realizing the consequences."

"She doesn't have a boyfriend." Once again tears formed on her lashes, and she blinked them back. She didn't have time to cry. "Not that I know of."

"Try not to panic, yet. She's only been unaccounted for the last few hours." Tye walked them past the desk sergeant. He handed Maggie a pad of paper and a pen. "Write down everything you learn. No detail is insignificant."

She grabbed his arm. "We'll find her, right?" The last word came out in a sob.

"We'll do everything we can." He looked at Jed. "Drive safe out there."

Jed's phone buzzed in his pocket and Maggie waited while he answered.

"Linc, what did you find out?" He nodded, "Nothing else?" He closed his eyes as if deep in thought. "We're with the sheriff now, I'll tell him. And our next step is to talk to everyone we can find in town and see if anyone saw anything." He paused again. "I'll touch base later."

"What?" Maggie had been focused on him during the entire phone call and he knew something.

"One day last week, Clint saw Susie driving one of the quads toward the entrance of the ranch. He didn't think anything about it at the time, but then Zak mentioned he'd been out mending a fence near the road and saw Susie talking to a guy in a gray truck."

Maggie's mouth went dry. "Was it a dually with tinted windows?"

"He didn't say, just that it was a late model, dark-gray truck."

"That's good information," Tye said. "When you're talking to shop owners, ask specifically if anyone has seen a truck fitting that description but don't mention the dual wheels straight up. Let's see what we can discover out first. Being that we're in ranching country, gray trucks are common."

"But when we add in the dual wheels and tinted windows, that is less so. A lot of cash tied up in a work vehicle."

"Unless that someone spends a lot of time driving long distance," Maggie said.

"What are you getting at?" Jed asked.

"Call the ranch and see if anyone can check to see if Susie's laptop is in the cabin. She has a horse sticker on the cover. If it's there, we need to get back to the ranch. She's been chatting with someone and I'll bet it was Cash. Don't ask me why I'm leaping to this conclusion, but it makes sense. She's become more argumentative since the fire, and she's talked about him more in the last month than she has in fifteen years. Then, there's her sudden interest in barrel racing and the rodeo. Who else could it be?"

"Talking to the man is one thing, but going someplace with him is another," Tye stated.

"That man could charm a snake. And if he wanted to, he could convince his own child of almost anything. But why now, after all these years of silence, would he be interested in being a part of her life and why not just ask to see her instead of going behind my back?"

Jed placed a calming hand on her shoulder and gently turned her so she looked at him. "We don't know that it's Cash, but if it is, he'll be easy to track down. Give Tye the particulars of his life with the rodeo and he can start investigating."

She nodded. "I can do that, and you'll call Linc again and ask about her computer?"

"Of course, and then we'll start with the shops closest to the library and fan out from there." He tipped up her chin. "I said it before and I'll tell you again, we will find her."

Maggie threw herself against his chest, fighting back the tears that wanted to flow. She held on with all she had, praying he was right.

28

*J*ed had gone into every store on Main Street that was still open with Maggie by his side. Most hadn't seen Susie or a gray truck except for a clerk at Claire's Closet. She described Susie and Cash perfectly. She remembered because they had been in just after ten, buying Susie a hat, scarf, and heavy gloves, and she called the man *dad*. He had been teasing her about being more like a city girl than a country girl. They had been laughing and having a grand time. So, that was good news that at least she wasn't kidnapped by a stranger.

Maggie was on the phone with the sheriff's office, relaying the information and told the desk sergeant they were on the way back to the ranch to see what information could be found on Susie's laptop. When she disconnected, she slumped in the seat. "I'm sorry about all of this. Having to be out in this storm helping me find my daughter—"

"You have nothing to be sorry about." He'd like to take her hand, but he clutched the steering wheel and drove slowly out of town. "Linc said he brought the computer up to the main house and Mary was fixing some snacks so we can make an action plan."

She sighed. "Now, I've stirred up everyone and Annie doesn't need this kind of stress being pregnant. We should take the computer back to my cabin and figure this out."

He glanced her way. "I'm not going to be the one to tell Annie she's too delicate to hatch a plan."

Her cell pinged and her heart pounded. "It's from Susie." She scanned the text message. "She said she and Cash are going on an adventure for the weekend and I shouldn't worry. She couldn't tell me ahead of time because, and I quote, 'Dad said you'd never let me go with him.'"

The truck skidded and Jed slowed down even more. He didn't need to call somebody to get them out of a ditch. "That SOB. You were right. Call Tye right away and he can put out an all-points bulletin and arrest him."

"He's her biological father. But wait, he signed away all legal rights and has never paid a dime in child support. That has to work in my favor, now." She dialed and said, "I need to talk to the sheriff."

Jed seethed and his gut was in knots. He wanted to take this guy and pound him into the ground for the fear he was causing Maggie, and manipulating Susie the way he had was unconscionable. *Cash had better hope Tye found him before I do.*

"That's right," Maggie said. "She's with Cash and I'm going to say he has a gray dually with tinted windows. Once I read her messages, hopefully it will have a clue where this big adventure is supposed to be happening."

He could hear the sarcasm in her voice, and he didn't dare take his eyes from the road. There had to be six inches of snow now and visibility was less than a quarter of a mile with the winds buffeting his truck like it was a tiny car. He had driven in storms before and was confident he'd get them back to the ranch safely; however, he was more concerned when they would need to go back out and get Susie. And as soon as he knew where she was, they were going.

Maggie finished her call with Tye. "They can track his

truck through his registration, but the most important piece of information is to find out where they might be headed. And he reiterated, this *is* a kidnapping. I'm going to have his butt thrown in jail for this stunt."

It was good to see the momma bear in her replace the fear. It had to be some comfort to know she was with Cash. "Why do you think he reached out to her now? Why not wait until she was eighteen or talk to you about seeing her?"

"Cash only thinks of himself. He was mad when I got pregnant, like I did it by myself. At first I was hurt he didn't want to get married, but now I'm glad we didn't. He hung around long enough to see if the baby was a boy or a girl. I think if Susie had been a boy, he might have stuck around longer. You know how some men want to raise a son to follow in their footsteps and all. But a girl didn't quite fit into his plans."

Jed had never understood how some men were hung up on having a son. If he had been that lucky, he wouldn't have cared. Son or daughter, he'd have been a hands-on dad. "It's his loss."

"But Susie missed out on having a father. She never came out and said anything, but things like the father-daughter dance at school? She was the only girl with her grandfather. Dad did what he could to fill in, but it wasn't the same."

A wind gust shifted the truck toward the edge of the road. Maggie sucked in a breath and grabbed the door, clinging to it, her knuckles white.

"We're okay, Mags. I'll get us wherever we need to go."

Her voice shook. "I know you're a great driver." Those were the last words she said until they turned onto the gravel road that led to the main house.

He was relieved to see it had been recently plowed so this part of the trip had been the easiest. He pulled under the portico and the front door opened before they reached it.

Annie was with Linc in the doorway. She drew Maggie into a hug. Linc clapped a hand on Jed's shoulder.

"Tough driving?"

Jed shrugged out of his jacket, being careful not to drip snow all over the hardwood floor. Using the boot jack, he pulled off his boots. It was an unwritten rule: no one walked on Mary's floors in boots and as far as Jed knew, even Pops hadn't dared to tread across the house in anything but socks or slippers.

Maggie was still in her heavy coat and Jed helped her out of it and then her boots. Once they were stowed, Annie ushered everyone into the oversized kitchen. A crackling fire warmed the space. Daphne set down a tray with coffee mugs on the table, and Mary placed an arm around Maggie, talking to her softly as she escorted her to a chair.

With Maggie under Mary's care, Jed turned to Linc. "A word?"

Linc walked down the hall and turned into the living room. "What's going on?"

"I need to blow off some steam and not in front of Mags. I can't freaking believe Cash Gordon would be talking to Susie behind Maggie's back and convince her to go on some stupid adventure with him. She's a smart kid; why would she do something like this?"

"I don't know how teenage girls think, but Annie said Susie's probably been building up this man in her mind to be a great person; she's just misguided, and when he reached out, she was so desperate for his attention she believed everything he said."

Jed clenched and unclenched his fists, trying to maintain control over his rage. "Didn't Susie realize how scared Maggie would be? They're so close."

"Susie used the word adventure—so she didn't give this a lot of thought. And didn't she say it was for the weekend? I'm betting she expected Cash to bring her home Sunday."

"Do you think he would have?"

"If he didn't have something convoluted going on, he would have talked to Maggie first."

Jed paced the length of the room, taking deep breaths while he centered himself. "I need to get back to Maggie so we can see what the SOB said to Susie."

"I know you're angry, but don't do anything you'll regret. Susie is going to need you and Maggie by her side when she realizes this wasn't the right thing to do."

"I'm not the girl's father."

"No, you're not. But I've seen the two of you and you've created a strong bond. Cash, at best, will disappoint her; at worst, destroy her—but you'll be her steady rock." He looked over his shoulder in Maggie's direction. "And she needs your strength, too."

"Thanks, Linc. I appreciate the pep talk. And you're right, they do need me as much as I need them."

Jed and Linc entered the kitchen again and Maggie had the laptop open. She didn't look up at anyone. "I have one more try for a password before it locks."

Jed asked, "What have you used?"

"Her birthday, my birthday, and I'm out of ideas."

He thought about what had been on her mind the most the last several weeks. "Is it possible she's changed it recently?"

Maggie nodded. "She's very careful and updates her password on her computer and phone every three months."

Jed thought that was ironic considering she went off with a man she didn't know but was worried about her passwords. "What about barrel racing. All one word."

Her fingers were poised over the keyboard. She looked at him. "I've got nothing to lose." Slowly, she typed the letters and hit enter. The smile on her face said it all; she was in. Her fingers now flew over the keys. "Nothing in her email, but she has her instant message open. That should give us something since the other day she was very secretive about it."

Jed didn't know if he should be looking over her shoulder or giving Mags privacy to read the threads. Annie and Daphne laid out plates of sandwiches, carafes of what was labeled coffee and soft drinks. He wasn't hungry and he was sure Maggie wasn't either, but he had no idea when they'd be able to rest so he fixed her a plate and set it next to the laptop.

"Look at this. He mentions he has a place in Sheridan, Wyoming."

Everyone in the room perked up. Jed pulled out a chair next to her and sat down. "Does it say where?"

She continued to scroll. "He's talking a lot about her barrel racing and that she'll be one of the best since she's inherited her love of horses from him and wouldn't it be amazing to have a father-daughter duo running the circuit." Smacking the table, she said, "He just poured on the flattery, and she lapped it up like a cat with a bowl of cream." She jumped up and paced the room. "It's not like I prevented him from seeing her; it was his choice. He didn't want her." She buried her face in her hands.

Annie and Daphne rushed to her side and wrapped their arms around her. Annie smoothed Maggie's hair back from her face. "You are a great mother and don't you second-guess that for one minute. When she gets home, the two of you will sit down and talk about this. But for now, you need to call the sheriff and give him the information about Wyoming."

Maggie looked at Jed. "I'm going to Sheridan; are you coming with me?"

His voice was soft but steady. "Where you go, I go."

Annie looked at Linc. "Get chains ready for the dually. They need a heavier truck than Jed's."

"You're not going to try and change my mind?" Maggie looked at her friends in a semicircle around her.

Annie placed a hand on her protruding tummy. "No. But

you're going to let us pack a cooler of food and drinks, and you're taking our truck. But that's after you call Tye Blackstone and tell him everything, including your plans."

Jed handed her the cell phone. "Time's a-wastin'." He liked this fierce momma bear side of her.

"Hello, this is Maggie Brady, and I know where Cash is taking my daughter."

aggie shivered despite the warmth in the cab of the truck. She was anxious to get away from this storm and start making real headway toward Wyoming. The roads were terrible. They had been driving for hours and so far, had just gotten out of Bozeman.

"Jed?"

He didn't look at her but said, "Don't thank me again, Mags. We're in this together."

She wanted to find the humor in something. "Are you reading my mind now?" His lips twitched. "I was going to ask if you wanted a sandwich yet."

Now he chuckled. "You were not, but I like the attempt at diversion. And no sandwich until I can at least see more than twenty feet in front of me."

Her cell rang. "It's the sheriff." Before it rang a third time, she answered and put it on speakerphone. "Any news? And Jed can hear you too."

"Good. Jed, where are you?"

"We're on ninety east, just coming into Livingston in maybe fifteen miles."

"Perfect. I'm right behind you. You're going to want to

head to the hospital in Livingston. Seems there was an accident. Susie is fine, just some bumps and bruises, but Cash is pretty banged up. The doctors know to hold him until I get there, and I've alerted local law enforcement to the kidnapping. They towed his truck, so he doesn't have transportation."

Maggie's heart was beating so fast she thought it might burst from her chest. "Tye, are you sure it's them?"

"Yes. Now don't start driving crazy just to get there. I'm less than thirty miles away. When you arrive, don't go inside without me. I want to keep this as calm as possible for Susie."

Clutching her heart, she said, "But she's hurt. I have to see her."

"And you will, but wait for me. Jed? Don't let Maggie go inside before I get there."

He glanced at her and then back to the road. "I'll do my best, but I think that's like trying to contain a momma bear protecting her cub."

In Maggie's mind, that was a good description. Susie was her first priority. "We'll be in the truck. We're driving the GSR dually; you can't miss it with the logo on the sides and tailgate."

"I know the truck. See you soon."

He disconnected and Maggie held on to her phone. "Maybe I should call Susie just to check in and make sure for myself she's okay."

"You'll see her in about an hour. She's safe, and isn't that all that matters?"

Jed reached for her hand and his touch calmed her. "You're right," she said.

"Why don't you call Annie and give her the update and make sure you tell them we should be home sometime tonight or early tomorrow morning."

He pulled her hand to his lips and grazed her knuckles. The warmth of his breath calmed her even more. She would never be able to describe how much it meant to her to have his support throughout this ordeal. She wouldn't have been able to be this strong without it. But that conversation was for another place and time.

"I'll put the call on speakerphone." She dialed and Annie answered on the first ring.

"Annie, good news. She's okay."

Maggie handed Jed a thick ham sandwich and opened a container of pickles and a bag of chips. The cooler was overflowing with enough food to last for days. She smiled when she thought of Mary and Daphne filling the cooler. They had thought of everything, including some of Mary's legendary cowboy cookies.

Jed had parked the truck so they had a clear view of the emergency department's door. No one was going to come or go without them being in plain sight. He was always thinking one step ahead.

She popped the tab on a can of cola and handed it to him. "Caffeine and sugar fix?"

He took a long drink and nodded to her empty hands. "Eat something. There's no telling how long we'll be in there or when we'll get home. You need energy to get through whatever comes next."

"My gut is churning. I'm afraid if I eat, it won't stay down." She saw the concern on his face. "Mary's cookies look good."

"Save one for me, please." He gave her a small smile. "Did you notice we drove out of the storm?"

"I'm taking it as a good omen." She nibbled on the cookie. Chocolate and nuts had never tasted so delectable. She chewed for a minute. "I want to wrap my arms around her and never let go and there is another side to me that wants to ground her forever."

"I'm sure both reactions are normal. But I'd stick with the hugging for now. You will need to talk about all of this and if she wants to have a relationship with Cash, I see a compromise in your future. Susie's interests will come first and you can put your past behind you. A man can change if he's motivated."

Taking half of a roast beef sandwich, Maggie devoured it. The cookie had kick-started her appetite. She was ready to eat the other half when her cell pinged with an incoming text. Her heart stopped.

Momma, can you come get me? I'm scared. I was in an accident with Cash and he's talking all crazy. I need you…

She handed her phone to Jed, then wiped her hand on a paper towel and picked up her handbag. "I'm going in."

Jed handed her back the phone. "Give me two seconds to call Tye. He can radio the police that are inside the hospital and make sure Susie is safe."

Maggie didn't want to wait, and if Cash was talking crazy, that wasn't a good sign. Maybe he had a head injury and he wasn't thinking clearly. She tapped the side of the door, unable to concentrate on what Jed was saying. Her only thoughts were sending strength to her child somewhere in that building.

"Got it." Jed pushed open his door. "Tye just pulled in and he's alerting the cops inside. We'll go in with him."

Finally, Maggie leaped from the truck and ran across the parking lot, only stopping long enough to make sure Jed was with her.

Tye opened the door to the emergency department and the three of them walked into an empty waiting area. He crossed the room and stopped in front of a man behind a desk. "Sheriff Blackstone. We spoke on the phone."

"Let me get someone."

"Where's Susie?" The fear that had subsided returned. And she jotted off a quick text.

I'll see you soon. XO.

A law enforcement officer strode in their direction. He walked up to Maggie. "Are you Maggie Brady?"

"Yes, I'm Susie's mother. Is she all right? I got a text from her a minute ago and she said Cash is talking crazy and she's afraid."

He looked at Tye. "He's been quiet every time we've gone in to discuss the accident. We should all go in together. Assess the situation and go from there. But one question, does Mr. Gordon have joint custody or visitation rights?"

"No, he walked out three days after Susie was born and we haven't seen or heard from him since."

With a brisk nod, he said, "Come with me."

*M*aggie clung to Jed's hand as the police officer led the way. Tye was behind them. The examination room was brightly lit, and Susie was sitting on the edge of a gurney. An older version of the man she remembered was lying on the other.

"Momma?" Susie's voice cracked and as she slid from the bed, Cash jumped up and jerked her back. Fear filled her eyes and the tears followed.

He sneered, "What are you doing here, Maggie? You just couldn't stand that Susie wants to spend some time with her dear old dad?"

Jed put pressure on her hand; could he feel her trembling? "When I heard she'd been in a car accident, I needed to make sure she was all right. You know, lay eyes on her for myself."

"I told Susie you had become the worst kind of mother:

overbearing, not wanting your kid to spread her wings. But she's got me, now."

Susie tried to wrench her arm from his grip, but the fabric of her chambray shirt pressed deeper into her arm as he tightened it. Dots of red seeped into the fabric.

"She's always had you, Cash. You just needed to reach out." Maggie took slow halting steps in his direction, and Jed kept the same pace. But the anger coming off Cash in waves was palpable.

"After that precious diner burned and you moved her to a ranch with strangers, I had to step in. No telling what those cowboys might do to my sweet angel." He nodded in Jed's direction. "I've been watching you and I see the way you've been looking at my kid."

"Let her go, Cash."

Jed's voice was low, and Maggie had never heard this tone before; flat and laced with anger. If they could keep Cash focused on them, the officers should be able to get into position where they could come between Cash and Susie.

"Mr. Gordon, please release your daughter. It looks like her arm is bleeding."

"I take care of my own. Not like you, Maggie. You were so careless, you left the fryolator on and burned your business and house down in one swoop."

"How did you know about the fryolator?" Maggie didn't need to ask any more questions. The horror of the situation had become crystal clear. "You jimmied the back door."

He grinned like a maniac. "Who knew you'd invest in good locks." His gaze darted around the room and stopped when he saw a tray of medical instruments. A gleam in his eyes only made his grin scarier. He lunged, dragging Susie with him, and grabbed what looked like an X-ACTO knife. He held it against Susie's collarbone.

The air whooshed from Maggie's lungs when she saw a prick of Susie's blood and heard her cry out. "Momma?"

"It's okay, honey. Your father is going to let you go." Maggie released Jed's hand and stepped closer, holding out her hand to Susie. "Let her go, Cash. If you wanted to hurt me, you have. But none of this is her fault."

"You're right, she didn't ask to be born. But she's here now and she's my daughter. You had her for the last sixteen years; she's mine for the next. We're going to ride the circuit together. She'll be the best barrel racer around. The accolades she'll win will be a direct result of me."

At this point both officers had their weapons drawn, pointed to the ground. Tye lifted his gun and said, "Mr. Gordon, release your daughter and we can see to her injuries and yours. No one will be doing any riding if we don't address them."

It was as if this was the first time he noticed he had pierced her skin. "Susie Q. I'm sorry that I hurt you." He ripped a package of gauze from the tray. "Here, use this."

Jed gave her a half nod and Susie took the bandage. She tore open the package and the gauze fluttered to the floor. As she bent to retrieve it, Jed ripped her from Cash's grip and twirled his body between them. With a warrior cry from Cash, the knife came down, slicing the back of Jed's neck.

Tye and the other officer rushed Cash, grasping his arm and smashing it against the wall, forcing the knife from his hand. Susie lunged at Jed and buried her head in his chest and Maggie followed. He held mother and daughter in the protection of his arms.

As the officers kept Cash's arms secured behind his back, Maggie heard Tye say, "Mr. Gordon, I'm placing you under arrest for the kidnapping of Susie Brady and for arson in burning down the Filler Up Diner." He proceeded to read Cash his rights.

Maggie cried, "Jed, you're bleeding."

"Mags, they need to take care of Susie first." He kissed the top of Susie's head and wasn't letting either of them go.

ed looked up as Susie entered the horse barn. He glanced at the clock on the wall and noticed it was almost four. Her shoulders were slumped, and she moved slowly as if the weight of the universe was resting on them.

Five days ago, they had made the drive from Livingstone and Maggie had ridden in the back seat on the trip home to the ranch. Mother and daughter had talked nonstop about how Cash had reached out to Susie, asking her to keep it a secret from Maggie, and all the lies he had told Susie about wanting a real relationship with her, but Maggie had prevented it. Cash had even gone so far as to say now that Jed was dating Maggie, she should be with him. Maggie would be fine. It had been sad to hear how that man had twisted so many things for Susie and her desperate desire to have a dad made it easy for him to manipulate her.

"Hi, Jed." She wouldn't look him in the eye; instead, her gaze landed mid-chest.

"Hello, how was school today?" He figured there was a burr under her saddle and she needed to work up to it in the conversation.

She kicked the hay on the cement floor, and he noticed she had her boots on. Maybe she was thinking of riding today.

"Okay. Everyone stopped asking about what happened."

"Good." He continued arranging the bridles on the hook even though he was done straightening them.

"How's Nahla?" She glanced in the direction of the mare's stall.

"Doing good but I bet she'd like an apple or carrot from you." He picked up an apple from the bench nearby and tossed it to Susie. She caught it like this was part of their normal routine.

"Um, Jed. Can I ask you something?"

He smiled and stopped what he was doing. He loved it when people started with that question. He didn't tease her and say she already had. "Sure. You can ask me anything."

She lifted her eyes and looked at the bandage that extended above his collar. "Does that hurt much?"

"Nah, it's just annoying. I'll go to the clinic at the end of the week and hopefully they'll take the stitches out."

"That's good." She shined the apple on her sweatshirt. "Why did you do it?"

Now she had his full attention. "Do what, Suz? Drive your mom to the hospital?"

"Well, that's part of it, but Mom said you were going to drive her all the way to Wyoming to get me, but then you heard about the accident and you went to the hospital."

"Why wouldn't I?"

"Was it because of Mom?" Her voice was timid, as if she was unsure of so many things in her life.

"Sure, your mom was part of it. But I wanted to come and get you and bring you home."

She looked him square in the eye. "Why did you shove me aside when Cash had that knife? You got hurt because of me."

He wanted to fold this girl into his arms but she wasn't ready. She needed to hear the truth from him. With any luck, the words would come out right. "Because as long as I'm around, no one will ever hurt you."

"What did Cash mean when he said he saw how you looked at me?"

"Susie, can we sit down and talk? I want you to hear what I need to say and if you want to have your mom here, that's fine, too. We can walk up to the dining hall and find her."

She thrust her chin up. "I don't need Mom, but I do need to know. What did he mean?"

Did he lead with how he felt about Maggie or how he felt about Susie? Looking at the confusion on her face, instinctively he knew. "In my heart, I know Cash was jealous of our relationship as I look at you as the daughter I never had. I would do anything to protect you. I will do anything to help you. And how I care for you has little to do with your mom, but so much more to do with our connection."

"How can you think of me like a daughter? We're not biologically related."

He walked to the door and when she wasn't following him, he stopped. "Come with me. There's something I want to show you."

They walked a short distance in the direction of the main house and Jed did a one-eighty and the entire ranch was spread out before them.

She leaned into him. "What are we looking at?"

"You tell me." He gave her a wide smile.

She popped her hands on her hips. "Is this a trick question?" When he didn't respond, she said, "Okay, I see horses, cows, people working, cabins, the dining hall, trucks, ATV, you know the ranch."

"Do you remember any of what Annie said on Thanksgiving?"

Her brow crinkled. "She's having a baby?"

He laughed. "Yes, she did say they're expanding the family. But she also said that the people on this ranch are a family. Each and every one of us that has chosen to live here, and for the record, other than you and your mom, no one has any biological connection. But we choose to live on this ranch and share our lives together. We work, eat, play, and live as a unit. Which we all consider our family."

Her mouth gaped open. "Annie said that Mom and I were the newest members of the GSR family." She gave him a playful punch in the arm. "I finally get it. Even though you fell in love with my mother, I filled a hole in your heart. You need me just like I need you."

He swallowed the lump that rose in his throat. "Something like that."

She tipped her head and gave him a thoughtful look. "Do you plan on marrying her?"

Dang, she was direct. So much like Maggie. "I'd like to, but we're not ready to make that commitment yet."

"Well, for what it's worth, you have my blessing to pop the question at any time and if you guys want to have a kid or two, I'm down with that." As she was talking, Jed could see her entire body relax and the old Susie from last week reemerged.

"Do me a favor and keep this part of the conversation just between us for now. I know you're not supposed to keep any secrets from your mom, but a proposal of marriage should be a surprise." He wasn't ready for Susie and Maggie to discuss wedding plans just yet. There was more to learn about each other and maybe he might be ready to take the plunge next year. But he wanted to make sure he would be a good husband and a good father figure to Susie.

She grinned and looped her arm through his and they started to head back to the barn. "Now that we've cleared the air and I know that you're basically my dad, let's talk barrel racing and that horse Ford is supposed to be finding for me."

Jed stopped mid step. "But wasn't barrel racing all about Cash?"

"In the beginning it was, but the more I've talked with Tate and rode Nahla, the more it's something that I want to do for me. Unless you think Mom won't let me."

"I can't speak for her, but there's only one way to know for certain. We're making a detour."

Susie laughed. "I know. We're going to see Mom and ask her."

He tweaked her nose. "And if she says yes, we'll call Ford when we get back to the barn."

Two weeks later, as the moon was beginning to rise in the east, a truck pulling a horse trailer parked in front of the barn, Ford behind the wheel. Susie and Jed waited outside and Maggie ran over from their cabin.

Susie was clasping and unclasping her hands. "I got her stall all set. I double-checked it when I got home from school." She nodded at the sliver of the moon. "Kind of fitting, don't you think?"

Maggie reached them and heard what Susie had said. "Kismet."

They walked around the back of the trailer, and Ford was unlatching it. "Susie, are you ready to welcome home your mare?"

Clapping her hands together, she grinned. "Moon Glow is going to fit right in."

Maggie squeezed Jed's hand when Susie said her name.

Ford said, "I'm going to unload her so why don't you stand to the side so she can see you as soon as she's clear of the trailer. Remember, she's smart and fast, but you two need to come together as a team."

"Got it." Susie moved to where Ford had pointed and he entered the trailer.

Jed could hear the mare paw the floorboards. She was anxious to get out, which matched Susie's eagerness. He stood at the ready in case he needed to take the lead rope, but he preferred that Susie take control from the first moment.

Ford was backing the mare out and the first thing Jed saw was the black tail followed by the prettiest silvery white coat and soon a black mane appeared, followed by her snout. Her name was fitting; she did look like the moon glowing against the night sky.

Susie stepped forward and stretched out her hand to rub her soft nose. "Hey girl, welcome home." The horse snorted and pressed her body against Susie, who couldn't smile any wider.

Ford handed her the lead line he had clipped on. "Let's take her into the paddock and she can stretch her legs for a bit. It was a long ride."

Susie clucked her tongue and the mare began to walk next to her. Ford stayed with them but let Susie handle the horse.

Maggie looked at Jed and it was easy to see by the expression she wore that she understood Ford had matched the girl and the mare perfectly. She asked, "So what's next?"

"Training with Tate."

Her laugh was soft and meant for his ears only. "Not with Susie but with us."

"A diner to reopen and lots more time together." He knew that wasn't what she was referring to, but were they ready for the next big step?

Maggie turned her back to the paddock and Jed stood in front of her. "Care to officially join our family?"

"Why, Maggie Brady, are you asking me to marry you?"

"Seems like I'm the one who has to make the first big moves in this relationship." She tipped her head. "You are the best man I've met and it's obvious to the entire world we're in love and there is a young lady over there who already considers you her dad. So, if you think I'm being pushy, I can wait and give you time to catch up to what is obvious. I love you, Jed Steele, and when I see the man standing in front of me who I want to be by my side for the rest of my life, I'm gonna ask the important question. Marry me?"

"On one condition."

She tipped her head and gave him a knee-knocking smile. "Name it, it's yours."

"That we build a house, have a barn for Susie's horse, and maybe think about having a couple more kids."

She stood on her tiptoes. "Kiss me."

Instead, he picked her up and twirled her in his arms. "I'm taking that as a yes." And then he kissed her.

The Following Fall

*M*aggie peeked out from the vestibule at the church. It was filled to capacity. The entire ranch and town showed up for this day. She couldn't help but smile looking at Susie standing at the altar with Jed, adjusting his bow tie.

Annie whispered in her ear, "Are you ready to go see your groom up close?"

They moved away from the door as Daphne walked up the aisle with purpose in her step. She was in her element as the wedding planner. She eased open the door. "What are you doing?"

"Just checking things out," Maggie said. "We have a full house and I happened to notice a very handsome cowboy was watching you earlier while you were adjusting the altar flowers."

"And who might that be?" Daphne looked over her shoulder.

Maggie tucked a lock of Daphne's hair back from her face. "Ford Shepard. When are you going to just ask him out? You know you want to."

Annie said, "You're interested in Ford? He's handsome, a

little broody, but I bet you could keep a smile on his face all day long."

Daphne adjusted the daisy crown Maggie wore in her hair. "We do not need to be talking about my love life when there is a groom waiting for his bride."

Maggie gave her a hug. "Then we'll revisit this when Jed and I get back from our honeymoon."

Waving her off, Daphne said, "Annie, are you ready to kick things off?"

With a kiss on her cheek, Annie smoothed the front of her dress. "Now, remember all you have to say is *I will.*"

The door eased open, and Maggie stood to one side as all eyes were on Annie. Daphne fluffed the back of her dress, and she began her walk down a short aisle. When Annie reached the altar, she turned and Maggie swore she gave her a wink. Well, wasn't that what friends were for, to keep you moving in the right direction?

Daphne went to fix something but dropped her hands. "You are a beautiful bride and I told the photographer to get a picture of Jed the moment he sees you."

"Thank you for everything."

Tears threatened to spill out, but Daphne said, "Nope, no time to fix your makeup." She waved her hands in front of Maggie's face as if to dry any tears.

"When it's your turn, Daph, I'll be right by your side." Maggie gave her a hug and said, "I'm ready."

It seemed like seconds when she took Jed's hand as he helped her up the single step to stand beside him at the altar. She scanned the people in the pews—no, they weren't just people, they were family.

Jed recited his vows, promising to be her steadfast and loyal husband for all time, and the pastor said, "Maggie, do you take Jed to be your husband, through good times and bad, be steadfast in your love for him for all time?"

She smiled at Jed, and winked at Susie. "I will."

LUCINDA RACE

BREATHE

Price Family Romance Series

CHAPTER ONE

The moment Tessa opened the heavy wood and glass door, her eyes were drawn to the tall, open stairwell. Kevin Maxwell leaned against the steel and glass banister, watching her.

He greeted her with a flat smile. "Good morning, Ms. Price. Welcome to Sand Creek Winery."

The glass door closed behind her with a small whoosh. She squared her shoulders and walked into her winery. "Please call me Tessa."

He gave her a half nod. "Tessa."

"I'm glad you're here. I wanted to talk with you."

"I've been clearing out my"—he gave a slow shake of his head—"your office. I won't be long."

She ascended the stairwell. "Wait."

Kevin's cool blue eyes met hers. He was dressed casually in a crisp, cream-colored shirt, the cuffs rolled back, which highlighted strong hands and muscled forearms. He had high cheekbones, a long, thin nose, and was more handsome up close. She guessed he was around her age.

"I'd like to start our relationship on the right foot."

His eyes never left hers. Challenging her.

She had been right that he wasn't thrilled to see her. She had negotiated the purchase through a broker since she suspected he wouldn't sell to a Price, no matter how much money was involved. She'd made a fair offer and he'd accepted it.

She pointed to an open door. "After you."

He did a one-eighty and strode through the doorway.

The large room was dominated by a long maple conference table and several leather chairs. In front of her was a wall of windows that looked out over acre after acre of vines. Pride surged in her. It already felt like she belonged. Several boxes were strewn about, in various stages of being packed. Not seeing a desk, she set her black leather briefcase on the table and walked to the windows.

"Quite the view." Kevin had come to stand next to her. He was so close, she could feel the waves of indifference radiating off him.

Without looking at him, she said, "It looks completely different from this perspective. The virtual tour didn't do it justice."

"When I built this building, my intent was to be able to look out and witness nature as it nurtures the vines. Watching the vineyard throughout the seasons gives me hope for the future. There's nothing like it." He turned away as if he couldn't bear to look any longer.

"Impressive." She was reminded of the view in Don's office. It was strikingly similar. She turned from the window and gestured to the chairs at the table. "Please, can we talk?"

He dropped to a wooden stool, leaving the executive chair noticeably empty.

Unsure where to start, she said, "You can trust me with Sand Creek Winery." She empathized with how it must feel, forced to sell his business.

When she sat down, he gave her a curious look. "It was

either accept the blind offer or let the bank take it. I'll admit if I had known it was a Price, I might have reconsidered."

She cocked her head to the side and let that comment slide. "I have a proposition for you." She wanted to rephrase that, but it was already out there.

His eyebrow rose and his chin dropped a fraction of an inch. "I'm listening."

"I would like for you to stay on as the general manager."

She could have heard a pin drop.

"And why would I want to do that?"

She leaned forward and clasped her hands, resting them on the polished wooden surface. "You're a good winemaker. I suspect a good marketing campaign can change sales. I happen to excel in sales and marketing."

"You think very highly of yourself."

She thought she saw a glimmer of humor in his crystal-blue eyes. "You know how to manage the field workers. You have a couple of excellent wines, but I want to hire an enologist to work with you, someone who is interested in growing this business."

Kevin leaned back in the chair and crossed his arms over his chest. "What's in it for me besides a paycheck?"

Available on all storefronts, *be sure to pick up your copy today.* **Order Breathe- Book 1**
Price Family Romance Series
Order Now

A FREE STORY FOR YOU

Have you enjoyed Moonlight Over Montana? Not ready to stop reading yet? If you sign up for my newsletter at www.lucindarace.com/newsletter you will receive Blends, the love story of Sam and Sherry, right away as my thank-you gift for choosing to get my newsletter.

Can two hearts blend together for a life long love..

His mother's final illness waylaid Sam Price's college dreams, but he's content working in his family's vineyard in a small town in upstate New York. When he finds a woman with a flat tire on a vineyard road, he's stunned to discover it's the girl he'd had a crush on in high school. He'd never been confident enough to ask her out back then. He'd been a farm kid. Her daddy was the bank president. Way out of his league.

Sherry Jones is tired of her parents' ambitious plans for her life. She'll finish her college accounting degree like they want, but how can she tell them about her real love: working with growing things? Then a flat tire and a neglected garden offer her an unexpected opportunity, with the added bonus of a tall, gorgeous guy with eyes that set her senses tingling.

What does a guy with dirt under his nails and calluses on his hands have to offer a woman like Sherry? It will take courage for her to defy her parents and claim her own dreams. Sam and Sherry's lives took different paths, but a winding vineyard road has brought them back together. Are they willing to take a chance to create the perfect blend for a lifelong love?

Blends is only available by signing up for my newsletter – sign up for it here at <u>www.lucindarace.com/newsletter</u>

LUCINDA RACE

BLENDS

a crescent lake winery novella

SNEAK PEEK

Chapter One

Early 1980's... Sherry Jones kicked the gravel road with the toe of her bright-pink sandal. Pebbles flew across the road to the scrubby grass on the other side. A flat tire and she was in the middle of nothing but grapevines. She turned three hundred and sixty degrees. As far as the eye could see, vines.

Why did it have to be so damn hot today? It was spring, not mid-July or August. A trickle of sweat ran down her back. Whether she went right or left, it was going to be a long, hot walk. She knew how far the gas station was from the direction she had come from, so it was time to go the opposite way. She couldn't remember ever being in this part of Crescent Lake before. Surely she'd find a house or a gas station that was closer down this road, and hopefully someone would be around so she could use the phone.

She jammed her keys in her distressed short-shorts pocket and walked at a steady pace. She hadn't gone more than a quarter of a mile when a blister began to form between her big toe and the thong. In the distance, she could hear the faint rumble of thunder, or was that a truck? If it was a storm, could her spring break get any worse? Last week, she broke up with Brad the cheater, her boyfriend of all of three months, and now she had to deal with a flat on her new used car, and a blister. She kicked off her sandals and walked in the sparse grass on the side of the road. There was a break in the never-ending field: another dirt road. The rumbling grew closer. A pickup truck slowed and came to a halt.

Her day just got worse. Arrogant and obnoxious, Sam Price stopped and leaned out the driver's window. "Well, look at you."

He flashed her a wide smile, his teeth even brighter against his tanned skin. She guessed it was from working outside all day. She hated to ask, but getting help was better than walking for miles, and it wasn't like he was the worst guy in the world. Just, they weren't friends.

"Hi, Sam." She shaded her eyes with her hand. "Any chance you know how to change a tire?"

"Sherry Jones, of all people to find wandering in my vine-yard; of course I do. You don't drive around in trucks all day without knowing how to do simple repairs." His smile was broad, and his tone was slightly cocky.

She put a hand on her hip and glared at him. "Well, not everyone drives around in trucks all day." She wanted to snap at him but if she did, there'd be no way he'd help change her tire.

"Touché." He shrugged. "I'm gonna take off. See ya around." He looked toward the road in front of him. With a wave of his hand, he dropped the truck into gear and eased forward.

She groaned. "Sam. Wait."

He turned to her. His lips twitched as the smile grew wide.

"I'm sorry. Is there any chance you have time to change my tire?" She jerked her thumb over her shoulder. "My car is back that way and the passenger side is flat as a pancake."

He propped his arm in the open window and pointed to the seat. "Hop in."

She tossed the offending thong in the truck and climbed inside. "Thanks. I appreciate you taking the time to help."

He gave her a sidelong look. "Why are you limping?"

"Blister. My sandals aren't made for walking any distance."

"Just for looks?"

Was that his way of paying her a compliment or was he being a smart aleck? "Something like that."

He threw the truck in reverse with a slight jerk and did a three-point turn to go back in the direction she had come from. She wasn't sure what to say to make small talk. They bumped over the dirt road without talking. He whistled off-key, and she stared out the windshield.

"Thanks again for helping. I'm sure you're busy."

"I've got time." He pointed to a car off to the side of the road. "Is that you?"

She nodded.

"Glad to see you pulled off the road."

Annoyance bubbled up. "Do you think I'd just leave it so no one could get around?"

He held up a hand. "It's a dirt road. Not many people come this way." He looked at her. "What are you doing out here?"

"Just driving around." The last thing she was going to tell him was the real reason she was driving through endless miles of grapevines. She was hiding from the world.

He pulled off and parked. "Pop the trunk so we can get the jack and spare."

He walked next to her. She couldn't help but notice he had grown taller since graduation but he still had those molten brown eyes, long eyelashes, and bleached-blond hair. Even though he had a hat and sunglasses on, she remembered them and him. He was easy on the eyes, and all the girls had thought so in high school.

She unlocked the trunk and the lid sprang open. He lifted up the tire well. It was empty. She felt the color drain from her face. Now what? No spare and she was stuck.

"Sherry, what are you doing driving around without a spare tire?"

She threw up her hands. "How should I know? I just bought this car when I got home for spring break. Don't they always have them?"

He flicked the trunk closed and leaned against it. He pushed his ballcap back and propped his sunglasses on the brim. His deep-brown eyes were fixed on her.

"Did you check the trunk when you took it for a test drive?"

Crossing her arms over her chest, she said, "No." She tilted her chin up.

"You can't assume when you're buying a used car." He kicked some stones with his work boot, causing little puffs of dust to float in the air. He looked down the road as if weighing his options. "Get your stuff and I'll drive you home. But I need to stop at my house first. You can use the phone to call a tow truck."

"I don't want to put you out. I'll call my mom and she can pick me up."

He seemed to consider what he wanted to say next and gave her a sidelong look. "I'll drive you into town. I need to go to the hardware store anyway." He walked around to the driver's door and opened it. "But the tow truck can be on its way out here and you could get your car back tomorrow. Leave the keys under the mat and we can get going."

She didn't move. "Are you sure the car is safe with the keys in it?" She pursed her lips. She had been saving for the last three years to buy her first car and she didn't want to have it stolen. Her hard work would have been for nothing if that happened. Besides, in two short months, she would need it to drive to her first full-time job.

"Out here, we'd leave our keys in the ignition with a flat. No one would bother it. Your car is safe."

She looked from Sam to her car. It wasn't that she didn't want to believe him but— "I'm not sure."

He extended his hand but it never contacted hers. In spite of that lack of touch, the racing sensation down her arm felt like he had. His voice softened. "Trust me. If someone steals your wheels, I'll replace it."

"Well, that wouldn't be necessary." She looked at him. It felt like it was the first time she was seeing Sam. It was a cliché, but if eyes were the window to the soul, this brash guy had a gentle side. "Alright." She took her bookbag and rolled up the windows and then placed the keys underneath and in the center of the rubber floor mat.

***

Sam waited for her before he walked back to his truck. "I have to swing by the house before we head into town. I need to get my list for the hardware store. Now, when we get to my place, don't worry about the dogs. They're big and bark a lot but they're harmless."

When he had seen Sherry walking barefoot down the dirt road, her shoulders slumped, he had to stop and help. She was the one girl he had wanted to date in high school but had never asked. She was out of his league. Her mom was a high school English teacher and her dad was the president of a bank in Syracuse. His family worked the land. Not that he was ashamed that his fingernails had dirt under them and there were calluses on the palms of his hands. They had a great life and he wouldn't trade it for anything, but she was out of his dating pool.

"When we get to the house, I'll get you something to put on your blister. You don't want to have it pop and get infected."

"Sam, you don't need to fuss over me." Her long blond ponytail swung from side to side. She looked like she was barely sixteen.

"How's college?"

"Two more months and then I have to start working full time."

He nodded as they drove. "Any ideas?"

"Office job. I'll have a degree in accounting, but it is so boring." She rolled her eyes.

With a chuckle, he asked, "Then why are you studying it?" He gave her a side-glance.

"My parents think it's a sound career choice. I might take the CPA exam."

"What's that?" He couldn't imagine not doing what he wanted to every day. It was like he had grape juice in his veins instead of blood. He loved the winemaking business. The ups and downs of a growing season, it was the ultimate thrill ride. This was something he wanted to do until he took his last breath.

"Certified public accountant." She released a heavy sigh. "I can become a controller for a company or something like that."

"I take it that's not for you." He saw the look of resignation on her face.

"I'll make a decent living, but doesn't it sound dull to go to an office every day for the next forty-plus years?"

Now he was curious. "What would you do if you could?"

She looked out the side window and waved her hand, trying to dismiss the question. "You'll laugh."

"Come on. Try me." Now he had to know. "If you tell me, I'll share a secret with you."

She gave him a curious look. He could tell she was trying to decide if she should or not.

"Landscape horticulturist."

It came out almost as a whisper.

She liked plants. He grinned. They had something in common after all. "Then why aren't you studying horticulture? Growing anything is gratifying." He pointed out the window to the passing landscape. "Look around you." The vines gave way to the long driveway leading to his parents' house. His mom always had beautiful flower gardens, but since she had passed away, they had become neglected.

Stately maple trees lined part of the drive as they grew closer to the house. "Don't look too close at the flower beds; they've been neglected the last couple of years."

Sherry's eyes were glued to them. Her eyes were bright as she saw the terraced gardens to the left of the road.

"Mom has, had, her vegetables there. She always had a huge garden and preserved a lot of what she grew. She also gave bushels of vegetables to the field workers each season." He smiled, remembering the baskets he'd have to lug down to the warehouses each afternoon after she harvested. Well, that was before he got involved with working in the fields to learn about the cultivation of grapes from Dad.

"Your mom doesn't garden anymore?"

"I guess you didn't hear." His hand tightened on the steering wheel and he swallowed the lump in his throat. "She died. Cancer." It still burned and probably always would.

She touched his arm with a featherlike gesture. "I'm sorry. I didn't know."

"It's just me and Dad now." He stopped the truck and looked at her. She curled her fingers into the palm of her hand. Silence filled the cab for the few moments they sat there. He could still feel the warmth of her touch.

He cleared his throat and mumbled, "Thanks." He pushed open the door. "Come on in."

She followed him to the back door. Two large German shepherds came racing around the corner at full speed. The scream died in her throat. They jumped against her and pushed her back. She stumbled. Sam put his arm out to catch her, but she still landed on her butt. They continued to bark. She cringed.

"Doc. Moe. Sit." Sam snapped his fingers. The barking ceased.

She was surprised to see the dogs' butts on the ground, and then they lay down, their heads resting on their paws. Sam extended his hand and pulled her to her feet.

"They won't hurt you."

In a few flicks, she brushed off her backside and straightened her top.

She glanced at them, suspicious. "Their teeth don't look harmless."

"They love people." He knelt on the ground and spoke quietly. Their ears twitched. "This is Sherry and she's my friend. Be nice."

She wasn't sure which dog was which, but first one's tail began to thump on the ground and then the other.

He looked up at her. "Do you want to pet them?"

She wasn't a dog person. Her parents had an old cat who spent her days and nights snoozing. Sherry was cautious but knelt on the ground in front of the dogs, feeling confident because of the way Sam looked at her. He had an intensity about him. Her pulse quickened and her eyes locked on his. "Okay," she breathed. But what she had just agreed to was anyone's guess.

Blends is only available by signing up for my newsletter – sign up for it here at www.lucindarace.com/newsletter

LOVE TO READ?

Cowboys of River Junction

<u>Stars Over Montana</u>
*The cowboy broke her heart but he never stopped loving her. Now
she's back ready to run her grandfather's ranch...*

Hiding in Montana
Can love flourish while danger lurks in the shadow?

Moonlight Over Montana
*Will a single mom find love with the handsome cowboy who saved
her and her daughter from danger?*

Orchard Brides Series
<u>Apple Blossoms in Montana</u>
*Twenty years later Renee and Hank are back where they fell in love
but reality is like a spring frost and is a long-distance relationship
their only option for their second chance?*

The Sandy Bay Series
<u>Sundaes on Sunday</u>

A widowed school teacher and the airline pilot whose little girl is determined to bring her daddy and the lady from the ice cream shop together for a second chance at love.

Last Man Standing/Always a Bridesmaid
<u>Barrett</u>
Has the last man standing finally met his match?

<u>Marie</u> *May 2023*
Career focused city girl discovers small town charm can lead to love.
The Crescent Lake Winery Series
<u>Breathe</u>
Her dream come true may be the end of his...
Crush
The first time they met was fleeting, the second time restarted her heart.
<u>Blush</u>
He's always loved her but he left and now he's back…the question, does she still love him?
<u>Vintage</u>
He's an unexpected distraction, she gets his engine running…
<u>Bouquet</u>
Sweet second chances for a widow and the handsome billionaire...

Holiday Romance
<u>The Sugar Plum Inn</u>
The chef and the restaurant critic are about to come face to face.
Last Chance Beach
<u>Shamrocks are a Girl's Best Friend</u>
Will a bit of Irish luck and a matchmaking uncle give Kelly and Tric a chance to find love?

A Dickens Holiday Romance
<u>Holiday Heart Wishes</u>
Heartfelt wishes and holiday kisses…

Holly Berries and Hockey Pucks
Hockey, holidays, and a slap shot to the heart.

Christmas in July
She's the hometown girl with the hometown advantage. Right?

A Secret Santa Christmas
Christmas just isn't Holly's thing, but will a family secret help her find the true meaning of Christmas?

It's Just Coffee Series 2020
The Matchmaker and The Marine
She vowed never to love again. His career in the Marines crushed his ability to love. Can undeniable chemistry and a leap of faith overcome their past?

The MacLellan Sisters Trilogy
Old and New
An enchanted heirloom wedding dress and a letter change three sisters lives forever as they fulfill their grandmothers last request try on the dress.
Borrowed
He's just a borrowed boyfriend. He might also be her true love.
Blue
Will an enchanted wedding dress work its magic one more time?

The Loudon Series
Between Here and Heaven
Ten years of heaven on earth dissolved in an instant for Cari McKenna when her husband Ben died.
Lost and Found
Love never ends... A widow who talks to her late husband and her handsome single neighbor who has secretly loved her for years.
The Journey Home
Where do you go to heal your heart? You make the journey home...

<u>The Last First Kiss</u>
When life handed Kate lemons, she baked.
<u>Ready to Soar</u>
Kate will fight for love, won't she?
<u>Love in the Looking Glass</u>
Will Ellie's first love be her last or will she become a ghost like her father?
<u>Magic in the Rain</u>
Dani's plan of hiding in plain sight may not have been the best idea.

Cozy Mystery Books
A Bookstore Cozy Mystery Series 2023
Welcome to Pembroke Cove, where witches and murders are multiplying...
<u>Books & Bribes</u>
It was an ordinary day until the book of Practical Magic conked Lily on the head causing her to see stars. And then she discovered her cat, Milo, could talk.

Catnap & Crimes
A witch, a snarky familiar and murder…

Tea & Trouble
When reading tea leaves turns to murder can Lily solve this latest case?

Scares & Dares
What does a haunted house and murder have in common? New witch Lily Michaels is determined to solve the case.

Holidays & Homicide

SOCIAL MEDIA

Follow Me on Social Media

Like my Facebook page
Join Lucinda's Heart Racer's Reader Group on Facebook
Twitter @lucindarace
Instagram @lucindraceauthor
BookBub
Goodreads
Pinterest

ABOUT THE AUTHOR

Award-winning and best-selling author Lucinda Race is a life-long fan of reading. As a young girl, she spent hours reading novels and getting lost in the fun and hope they represent. While her friends dreamed of becoming doctors and engineers, her dreams were to become a writer—a novelist.

As life twisted and turned, she found herself writing nonfiction but longed to turn to her true passion. After developing the storyline for A McKenna Family Romance, it was time to start living her dream. Her fingers practically fly over computer keys as she weaves stories of mystery and romance.

Lucinda lives with her two little dogs, a miniature long hair dachshund and a shih tzu mix rescue, in the rolling hills of western Massachusetts. When she's not at her day job, she's immersed in her fictional worlds. And if she's not writing romance or cozy mystery novels, she's reading everything she can get her hands on.

www.ingramcontent.com/pod-product-compliance
Lightning Source LLC
Chambersburg PA
CBHW061240210726
48293CB00003B/843